D0398044

The Catch Colt

MARY O'HARA

The Catch Colt

McClelland and Stewart

First published in Great Britain 1979
by Methuen Children's Books Ltd.

The Canadian Publishers
McClelland and Stewart Limited
25 Hollinger Road, Toronto M4B 3G2

CANADIAN CATALOGUING IN PUBLICATION DATA

O'Hara, Mary
    The catch colt

Based on the author's musical The catch colt,
published by Dramatists Play Service, 1964.
ISBN 0-7710-6843-3

I. Title
PS3529.H37C37 1981   813'.52   C81-094231-3

The musical version of *The Catch Colt* is available for
production through Dramatists Play Service, New York.

Printed and bound in the United States of America

Chapter One

The Great Plains of America, about one-third of the width of the continent going west from the Atlantic seaboard, are hundreds of miles in extent. They are bounded on the west by one of the highest mountain ranges in the world, the Rocky Mountains. It runs from north to south through the entire continent like a jagged backbone – the Continental Divide.

Here is the American 'West', backdrop of Wild West stories read and enjoyed the world over.

It is strange that those tales should be about killings, bandits, outlaws, gunmen, when the land itself is so serene, so silent, and so incredibly beautiful. A vast expanse covered with a rippling sea of grass, bright emerald green. Sky, a deep cobalt blue, in which float huge sculptured clouds, dazzling white, casting purple shadows on the plains.

All movement is slow and dreaming. The clouds drift. The shadows change their mysterious shapes. A faint wind blows from the west, never ceasing.

A car travelling all day long on the old dirt trails that crisscross the plains, never varying its fifty miles an hour pace, would face the same vista at the end of the day as at the beginning.

A hidden world with a slow heartbeat. A world of heavenly colour, of loveliness, magical and spellbinding.

These are the Great Plains.

They rise to an elevation of eight thousand feet at

Spurling,Wyoming, where the land falls away again to a wide valley, big enough to hold the town of Laramie and the University of Wyoming. After that it rises again, climbing towards the Rocky Mountain Divide. Its towering peaks, snow-covered most of the year, mingle with the clouds.

The Divide, however, is not impenetrable to further travel west. At its base, tunnels and passes cut and twist their way through the rock. They descend, little by little, to deserts and flowering orchards, to old Spanish Missions full of art treasures and at last to the long, cool combers of the Pacific Ocean.

The Wyoming night sky demands special mention, the stars are not mere specks of light shining and twinkling and keeping their places in the familiar constellations, but small globes of blazing white fire, close to each other, shouldering each other, crowding the sky from horizon to horizon.

Readers of American wild west thrillers are familiar with such terms as bronco-buster, wrangler, cowpuncher.

Joey Bud was a cow-puncher, a tall good-looking fellow with deep blue eyes the exact shade of the larkspur that dots the plains, under dark brows that had a lift at the outer corners like a hawk's wing. Hair and skin were the same colour, tan. He thought he was about twenty but could not be sure because he had no family to keep track of his birthdays.

Joey had never gone to school. And his unique way of dealing with the English language even suggested that he could not read. He doubled his negatives as if it was a duty. He substituted one word for another. Eff'n for if. Allers for always. Dinn for didn't. He altered vowel sounds at will, omitting the final 'g' from every 'ing'. His speech was quaint, all his own, and not unpleasing.

In spite of his lack of schooling Joey did have knowledge of a sort, and a good deal of it, gained as those always gain it, who live close to nature and are alert to observe and understand her signs.

Roy, his horse, was a fine schoolmaster, particularly Roy's ears. They were long and finely shaped, the ears of a thoroughbred, and they caught every message the air waves brought, turning every which way, sometimes together, often separately.

The great mountain range, the Rockies, lay directly ahead, perhaps a hundred miles away. Joey could see those shimmering peaks soaring up against the sky. Sometimes he could smell the snow. An icy breath, delicious and sweet, mingled with the pine and sage of the plains.

Joey knew that horses can see much farther than men and wondered what the difference was. For sometimes it seemed to him that Roy was intent upon what was happening on those mountains. Was he actually seeing something? Perhaps an eagle's sky-high flight carrying a whole sheep in his talons, planning an easy kill; drop the sheep, follow it down and feast at leisure? Or was he just listening? Perhaps to the thunder of an avalanche, or the whistling fury of a gale rising to a scream?

When Roy shied it was sure to be at something close by. Joey would look down and see the snake slithering off a rock. And there were always the big jack rabbits. One would burst out of his burrow almost underfoot, propelled by the piston-like thrust of his powerful hind legs. The great leap would throw him on the wind to sail like a blown tumbleweed. At which Roy would take a great leap himself, then attempt to excuse it with an angry snort and toss of his head.

7

But between the close and the far away there was a whole world of interest. Those small bands of moving creatures were antelope and deer. The animals which preyed on them – wolves, coyotes and mountain lions – hid themselves well, but Roy spotted them. And Joey would know by the horse's sudden change of gait, his head swung around to search, the tension in his whole body, that something of danger was near.

And there were, of course, the wild horses. They were as familiar a sight to westerners as chickens to a farmer. They roam the open range of Wyoming singly or in bands, and, when caught and trained, have become the American cowboy's 'mustang' or cow pony.

Since their inheritance goes back to the full-blooded Arabian steeds brought from Spain to Mexico centuries ago, quite often there are throwbacks of such beauty, power and intelligence, they take the breath away.

Such a one was Roy. He was taller than most mustangs, standing nearly sixteen hands, gleaming blue black with flowing tail and mane, four white socks on his slender ankles and a crescent-shaped blaze between his large intelligent eyes.

To learn all that a horse could teach, was a world of knowledge, but only a beginning. One also had to learn from human beings and this, Joey had found, was much more complicated because of words. If there are too many words you get no facts from them at all. Then you have to look for signs here too. Look into a horse's eye and you instantly know if you can trust him. Most animals can be trusted if they are not frightened. But a man? He is two-faced. He is indeed two men. Trust one and the other will betray you. But play safe by mistrusting all, shutting yourself up against all and you may miss the one who would give you not only the simple facts but truth and wisdom as well.

There are not many of these. You know them usually when you look back. They stand out.

There was one such whom Joey remembered. He thought of her as *Thet ole Granny*. She had a niche in his memory and he could summon a mental picture of her at will. A little old woman dressed in cap and apron seated in a rocking chair, knitting. She taught Joey folk songs in a cracked old voice, told him tales which she said came out of the Bible. She taught him how to judge men. How you could tell a wrong 'un by the smell of his sweat. Or one you had to obey by a certain ring in his voice.

'When you meet one of those, Joey, never sass him. Don't even answer back. Just do what he says.'

So to the teaching of Roy was added the homely and earthy knowledge of the old Granny.

Chapter Two

Wyoming sheepherders have acquired a curious repu-
tation in the West and are talked about a good deal.
They have become almost legendary characters.

In so humble an occupation one would expect them
to be simple men, indigenous to the soil. And many
are. But others, say the stories, are nothing of the kind.
They are runaways from the big Eastern cities;
notables who have got into trouble with the law, must
disappear immediately, get as far away as possible and
never return.

Once arrived in the far reaches of the Wyoming
sheep country they fall in love with the life. A life of
outdoor activity, an occupation easy to learn, the sheep
themselves and the glorious country – all delights
them. It was escape! Freedom from the rules and
conventions of polite society in matters of dress and
general behaviour, and particularly freedom from
their former associates.

There was an old sheepherder called Windy who
was also a refugee from the East though for quite
different reasons. He had once been a lecturer at
Harvard University and his real name was Joseph
Gerard Willoughby.

If he had not already acquired his nickname of
Windy when he lectured, he might have acquired it
subsequently, when he found himself near Wind River
or in the little Wyoming town of Windemere.

No one ever knew him as anything but Windy. It

was quite a tragic story which had brought him to Wyoming.

Long ago when he had been on the Harvard faculty, he had raised his son, an only child, very carefully. He was a widower and had to be father and mother both. His hope was that the boy would follow in his own footsteps and eventually be teaching at Harvard. All went well until a certain girl came along. Joseph disobeyed his father by marrying her; disobeyed him again by dropping out of college. Then the young pair disappeared.

A year later the Professor had received a letter postmarked Windemere, Wyoming. It said that the young wife had died giving birth to a baby boy. That he had named him after his father and himself, Joseph Gerard Willoughby, the third.

The Professor wrote the name in the family Bible and thought that Joseph would come home now with the little boy and perhaps take up his work in college again. Of course he would forgive him and welcome him. But Joseph did not ask forgiveness. He did not even write. After a few years the Professor fell seriously ill and had to retire.

At last it came to him that if sons will not return and beg their father's forgiveness, then fathers must seek out their sons.

So he went to Windemere, registered at the smalltown hotel and made inquiries. Soon the report reached him that a man answering to Joseph's description had died of tick fever in a sheepherder's camp somewhere outside of Windemere. The man had a little boy with him.

But all that had been several years ago. No sheepherders were running sheep now anywhere near Windemere and nothing at all was known about the little boy.

The Professor was profoundly shaken. It was as if he had never realized that time was always secretly changing things. From day to day they changed, almost unnoticeably. Death, too, was standing by, watching the game, able at any moment to tip over the board and end it. There was now nothing left to the Professor but the hope of finding the little boy, his grandson.

So began his long search, the wanderings from ranch to ranch, the persistent queries, 'Have you seen a little boy? A little fellow about so high? Blue eyes? A tow-head?'

He was not alone as he searched, for, in a sense, a desired object is already in one's possession. Sometimes he could feel the little boy's hand in his.

He visited the sheep camps of those ranches which ran a few sheep as well as other livestock, where the herders lived close to the earth, sleeping in their wagons and moving from place to place. Surely the word would be passed if anyone had seen a little lost boy.

Jepson Heath's great ranch was one of these, running sheep but famous particularly for his pure bred Guernsey milch cows.

Windy made no change in his personal fastidious habits but wore the handsome buff corduroy uniform of the Montana herders, inherited they say from Basque immigrants.

It was an entirely new life for the Professor and one in which he found increasing pleasure. And how it agreed with him! Every vestige of illness and frailty had left him. The springy turf underfoot, the intoxicating air, the beauties of the scenes his eyes feasted on, the empty days, the simple people, the animals – all delighted him.

He never wearied of watching the lambs as they 'skipped', shooting four or five feet straight upward, then reversing and coming down headfirst in a perfect jack-knife dive.

Windy's old life became dimmer and less real until, at last, it seemed never to have existed at all.

In time Windy became a sort of legend in Wyoming. Dignified, almost famous. All this created a sort of dream existence which had power over him and was strangely satisfying – indeed almost a way of life.

Chapter Three

Before her marriage to Jepson Heath, Martha Combs had been a school teacher and a very brilliant one. So Letitia, their daughter and only child, was able to acquire a fine education without leaving home, which suited the child right down to the ground.

She was an apt pupil and an avid reader. She received the customary schooling, familiarity with the French and English classics, the three Rs and knowledge of the world's geography. But Martha added other subjects, keeping the accounts of a working ranch and the care of the milking utensils, their cleansing and sterilization.

The layout of a large ranch usually includes many miles of grazing land, leased from government or railroad. This surrounds a nucleus of property owned outright. At the core of this is the owner's home and all the other buildings necessary for the working of a ranch.

On the Heath Ranch all the buildings were substantial. The bunkhouse was a two-storey log house big enough to accommodate a dozen hired hands. The spring house, near it, was made of stone, much smaller, with a trough running around the inside where buckets of fresh milk standing in the cold running water were always ready for use in the bunkhouse.

Between the two a narrow twisting path led to higher grazing land and upland pastures.

Below bunkhouse and spring house was a clearing, an acre or more in extent, levelled and turfed like a village green.

On the edges of the clearing were the other buildings, tool house and shop, smoke house and storehouse. On the far side a wooded hill, almost a cliff, overhung it. And lastly, on the lower edge, was the barn, an immense and ancient structure which extended the full width of the clearing to the cliff opposite and formed a barrier between the ranch buildings and all that went on there, and the open meadows below. It was several stories high. Its differing roof lines, peaks and gables, gave it the outlines of a small cathedral. Inside it was divided into pens, rows of stalls and corridors, roomy enough to shelter dozens of cows and calves, hundreds of ewes and lambs through the winter storms.

The family mansion, as handsome and commodious as any city dwelling, stood just across the road from the barn and completed the ring of buildings.

It was customary for big Wyoming ranchers to send their children to fashionable boarding schools in the East for their education. But Jepson and Martha Heath could not bear to let their daughter go so far away. And she begged to stay home. She loved the ranch. All those rich meadows and grazing lands and pastures were her own private domain and she the reigning princess. She was sure that not even her parents knew the land as well as she, little faraway glens and dells, entrancing hidden spots.

There was one where a spring formed a pool among ferns. Out of it poured a stream, not much wider than her own slim body but surprisingly swift. This she had chosen as her own special bathing spot.

Facing upstream like a trout, stretched at full length, she would lie in it on hot summer days, revelling in the delicious coolness. Her elbows planted in the sandy bottom, her small heart-shaped face cupped in her hands and her long yellow hair floating back on the current. Her clothes – blouse and skirt, small white panties – lay on the bank.

Sometimes she reversed the trout game. Instead of being one herself she would bring a nice catch home in a basket. She knew just where to find them.

A tiny stream ran along the upper side of the long irrigated meadow below the ranch buildings, twisting, almost tying itself in knots. At every corner, deep under the bank, was apt to be a square-tailed rainbow trout, six or eight inches, sometimes ten or twelve. Cooked out-of-doors, slightly smoked, Jepson Heath loved these beyond anything.

Letty's secret hiding places were between the bales of hay in the third-storey hayloft of the barn. If she had an exciting book just come from the library, she could read it in peace here. Or, if there were boring visitors coming to call, there was a place no one would ever think of looking, a five-branch crotch in the old sycamore tree, invisible from below. Or she might be close by behind the spring house seated on an upturned orange crate. Or even inside the spring house having a cosy chat with Jim Billings, her trusted confidant.

The years passed happily and swiftly. Martha and Jepson began to think about Letty's companions. Who would they be in this isolated place? What social life could she have here? She was eighteen, already of marriageable age. Who would win her? She had often wondered herself.

Girls were given hope chests and taught to fill them with house linens and embroideries. Even encouraged to make garments suitable for a layette.

Boys were taught to be strong; able to fight to defend their women. They also had to be good workers so they could provide a home for wife and children and maintain it properly.

Girls were warned against being flirtatious, at least against appearing so. But there were ways to circumvent this and still ask and answer the same all-important question. Casualness. Playing games together, in fact, doing anything together could provide a very smooth mask.

But Letty was not smooth. She was a child of nature, simple and somewhat shy. To look directly into the eyes of men was more than flirtatious, it was provocative and inviting. Letty's whole instinct was against it and she never did it. Never, that is, until she looked directly into the eyes of Joey Bud and could not look away.

This is how it happened. She woke early one morning and even as she stretched and yawned, she noticed that her room was lit with sunrise colours. The tall casement windows, angled back, were wide open.

She slipped out of bed and crossed the room to stand between them looking at the pink and gold clouds in the sky.

Then a horseman rounded the bend in the path that skirted the side of the house below her window. And she looked down and he looked up. Their eyes met.

He stopped his horse.

Chapter Four

One day before sun-up in early June, Jim Billings was standing at the corner of the spring house. His white chef's cap was already on his head, his butcher's apron belted around him. He was carrying a one-gallon canister of milk. He needed it for breakfast.

He stood there for a moment, looking down across the clearing at the cow barn and the road that came in from the meadow because he had heard a horse trotting.

When he first heard the horse, its gait had been sort of ambling single-foot. Then it had suddenly stopped dead. That must have been below the family dwelling just before making the right angle turn to enter the ranch. The horse had stayed there for a long minute or two, then resumed progress.

It was still dark but sunrise colours were flowing over the sky and the few remaining stars were going out, one by one.

Presently a horseman rode in and stopped between the ranch house and the cow barn. He was just a blacker shadow against the darkness and Jim could not tell if the rider was a man or a boy until he dismounted, stepping easily out of the saddle, swinging one long leg over the pony's haunches.

He stood tall on the ground and Jim decided that he was young and had probably come looking for a job.

There was a haystack near the barn. The rider led

his pony to it then turned back and looked up at the second-storey windows of the Heath House.

He stayed so long without moving that Jim was puzzled.

Then, as if sensing that he was being watched, the stranger turned and they faced each other, though at a considerable distance.

'Howdy, stranger,' called Jim and they started toward each other, slowly.

'Howdy. This the Heath ranch?'

'That's right. You looking for a job?'

'Yup. Any chance?'

'The Boss keeps six Boys the year around.' (Hired hands were called Boys no matter what their age.)

'How about a haying crew?'

'We've already taken on some extra men. But it's a heavy crop. We might need more. Say! Better take your pony off the haystack. We're short of hay till the new crop's in.'

The stranger stopped where he was.

'I seen the stack was et clear down. Whereabouts will I put him?'

Jim pointed. 'See that bit of white fence at the far corner of the barn? There's a gate at the end of it you can lead your pony through. There's a good little fenced pasture beyond. The calf pasture.'

The stranger did as he was told but when he returned, instead of going around by the gate, came over the three-rail fence in an easy vault.

'Spry,' thought Jim, sizing the young man up, still puzzled by the interest he had shown in those upstairs windows.

'Say – why'd you stand there staring up at that window so long?'

After a moment's hesitation, Joey answered the question with another question, 'Whose room is that?'

'It's Letty's. The Boss's daughter. Why what's the matter with you? You look as if something had struck you all of a heap.'

'Nuthin'. I'm aw right.'

'You been riding all night?'

'Jess about.'

'Well, you're hungry. That's the trouble. Sorry I can't give you breakfast yet. Not until Hank gets back. He's up at the stable graining the horses.'

'Who's Hank?'

'Hank Burrows. The foreman here. He's the one will give you the job. If you get it. But I can give you some coffee. Come on up to the bunkhouse.'

They walked together to the bunkhouse.

Inside, the stranger hung his hat on a rack near the door.

'Sit down.' Jim pushed the young man into a comfortable chair. 'I'll have some hot coffee for you in a minute.'

He went to the stove, shook up the fire and poured in a scuttleful of coal, then a handful of kindling. It began to crackle and blaze.

The visitor had not moved. He sat where he had been put, staring, still in a daze.

The room was like most old-fashioned kitchens, large and homelike. To the left of the door the big iron stove fitted into an alcove that occupied nearly half the wall. At right angles to it was a long narrow dining table.

The rest of the room was furnished for comfort. There were a few armchairs, a couple of benches and a number of the sturdy wooden chairs called captain's chairs.

There were decorations on the walls. One of the many Boys who had used the room had displayed a talent for drawing – they were mostly sketches of women with shapely figures. Most prominent were the female portions of the female figures.

A string of sleighbells hung there too, and a pair of chaps, some bits of harness.

Sleeping quarters were upstairs, reached by a flight of steep narrow stairs.

The coffee was steaming. Jim filled a thick china cup. 'Here's your coffee. Strong enough to make your hair curl. What's your name?'

'Joey Bud.'

'Cream and sugar?' Jim proffered them and Joey helped himself.

Jim got out a big yellow mixing bowl and broke eggs into it.

'Joey Bud?' he said. 'I don't know the name. Where's your home?'

'Ain't got none.'

'I mean – who's your folks?'

'Never had none. I'm a loner.'

Jim stirred and beat his batter. 'Tell you something, Joey. There's no such thing as a loner. Every single person that ever was born or ever will be is hitched to someone else. Ever think of that?'

Joey said, 'Then they musta lost me or laid me down some place and fergot to pick me up agin, cuz I never knowed one on em.'

'But you must have known *of* them,' argued Jim. 'Because of your surname. Bud. Who's the Buds?'

'They ain't no Buds,' said Joey. 'That ain't a real name. Wen I seen everbuddy had two names I jess tuk it of myself. Only name I got a real right to is Joey.'

Jim was startled. 'You mean – you don't really know who you are? Your pa and ma not wed? Like a catch colt?'

'I've been called that plenty of times.'

'But you're not sure of it?'

'Not sure of anything.'

'Who took care of you when you were a little tyke?'

'Lotsa people. Ranchers. Anybody'll take in a kid eff'n he kin do chores. Fill the kindling baskets; carry swill to the pigs; or milk. As fur back as I kin remember I bin settin' under cows, milkin'.'

Jim went on preparing breakfast at the same time quizzing Joey with the zest of an amateur detective.

'But think way back, Joey. At the very beginning of your life. What can you remember?'

But Joey shook his head. 'Just bits and pieces. It's all foggy except that dawg.'

'What dog?'

'I had a dawg oncet. He wuz yaller. I called him Yaller Dawg. We slept on the floor together and in the night he'd lick my face.'

Joey took several gulps of his coffee and added reminiscently, 'Sometimes, even now, I kin feel them licks.'

Jim was standing still, interested, staring at Joey. 'And—,' he prompted.

Joey suddenly laughed. A wide grin flashed across his face showing big square teeth, very white and even.

'In the daytime we had fun,' he said, 'chasin' chickens together.'

Jim was setting the long table with crockery and cutlery. 'But say. If you had to take a name – why Bud? Why not a name with class?'

Joey answered, 'One day a fellow said to me, "Lend a hand here, Bud."'

Jim stopped and stared. 'But they say that to every boy.'

'That's jess wot makes it mine as much as anybody's.'

Jim still stared.

'Eff'n I'd chose a name with class an' said it was mine, that 'ud be cheatin'.'

Jim stood quite a long time and when he spoke his voice was different. Very gentle and kindly. 'I see what you mean.'

He went to the stove and did some cooking, got one of the big plates, piled it with food and brought it to Joey.

Joey looked up and again the big grin put a white slash across his suntanned face.

'Oh, thanks.' He took the heaped plate and began to eat. Jim watched him.

'I've been thinking. You'd better get out of here. Fill yourself up first.'

Between mouthfuls Joey said, 'I gotta scram? Why?'

'Hank'll be down here soon and he'd better not see you.'

'Thought he wuz the one who'd hire me.'

'He won't hire you. Not with that face.'

'What's wrong with my face?'

'You're a looker – that's what's wrong with it. Hank's a looker himself. And he aims to be the only one around.'

'Wot's faces to him? Foreman of a big ranch like this?'

'He's sweet on Letty Heath.'

'They engaged?'

'Hank says yes.'

'Takes two, don't it?'

'She sees him every day. He drives her to barn dances in his car. And he's got her parents on his side. They think the world of him. Besides, he's a graduate of the agricultural college, Wyoming State University at Laramie.'

The light went out of Joey's face and he ate his

breakfast without tasting it. When he finished, he stood up and handed the plate to Jim.

Jim took it. 'Had enough?'

'Plenty. Mighty good grub.'

'Now listen to me. Go down to the milking barn and hang around there. When the milking's over the Boss weighs the milk. Then he's likely to come out. Then's your chance. Ask him for the job. Now *git*!' And Jim practically pushed Joey out of the door.

Just in time, for as Joey walked across the clearing he heard voices at a distance behind the bunkhouse. One had carrying power. It was harsh and grating and peremptory, as if accustomed to giving orders. That was probably Hank Burrows.

As Joey neared the milking barn a big man emerged from it. He was the same height as Joey, over six feet, but twice his girth without being at all fat.

'Good mornin', Mr Heath. 'I heered you was goin' to put up your hay and thought you might need an extry man.'

Jepson Heath's eyes went over the young man appraisingly, measuring his muscles and strength.

Heath lifted his head and roared, 'Hank!' The big, booming voice matched his proportions.

'Coming!' came the answering shout.

Heath turned again to Joey. 'Where you been working?'

'Haskell's,' said Joey. 'Jess finished.'

'Good crop.'

'It sure was. Hay's thick this year.'

Hank was beside them, glancing at Joey.

'Hank,' said Heath, 'here's the extra hand we need. I know you're full up in the bunkhouse. Put him in the space above the tack room in the horse stable. There's a cot there already and room enough. He can put his pony out back in the wooded pasture above the horse stable. Give him his orders. He's all yours.' And Heath stalked off in the direction of his own house.

The two young men faced each other. Joey started to lift his hand, but when Hank stood rigid, dropped it again.

'I'll use you tomorrow in the hay field,' Hank said. 'For today, get settled in. The Boss told you where. Stow your gear and learn your way around this ranch, every turn and twist of it.'

Jim Billings' voice shouted from the bunkhouse, 'Come and get it!' And there was the loud clattering of two pans simulating a breakfast bell.

Men converged on the bunkhouse from all directions.

Hank Burrows turned and walked away.

Chapter Five

A few hours later the door of the ranch house opened. Letty came out and stood looking around in a state of excitement.

It was a windy day. Her short pink skirt was fluttering. The sky was full of clouds, some of them quite dark and all of them moving swiftly. It looked as if there would be a storm before night.

Having examined the sky she resumed her search. She was looking for someone and made a painstaking survey but there was no one to be seen in the clearing or near any of the buildings.

Then she saw the horse.

Letty knew all the horses on the ranch. This was a strange horse. It was quietly grazing in the little pasture behind the rail fence at the far end of the barn.

Letty ran across the clearing, bare brown legs flashing. She went up and over the three-rail fence like a squirrel and stopped abruptly on the other side. The horse had whirled around to face her. She didn't want to frighten him.

As if she could learn something about the owner by looking at his horse, she remained motionless for a few moments, then she heard the voice behind her.

'Mornin, Miss.'

She was so startled, her breath left her.

She turned.

'Oh – good morning.'

There he stood, on the other side of the fence, his hat held in his left hand as he spoke to her.

'Good morning,' she said again as if she had not said it before, then took a step forward and held out her hand. 'I'm Letty Heath.'

They touched hands so briefly it seemed as if they were afraid. Her heart was pounding. She felt faint and put her right hand on the fence to steady herself.

He kept his eyes on her and let his hat fall on the ground.

'Then it was you – on your horse – under my window—' she gasped.

'Yup.'

She stood silent, her head drooping, not looking at him. She ought not to have said that, she thought, but what was the use of pretending? Something had happened. And it felt like something big and important. Would she ever be the same again? He must know it as well as she. But she went on pretending and trying to cover it up.

'I couldn't see you very well,' she muttered without looking at him.

He answered, 'I cud see you very plain, standin' up there in your window, lookin' down at me.'

There was a long silence while Letty clutched the fence and wondered what was happening to her.

His voice went on, 'And it seemed to me I recognized you.'

'But how could you? You've never seen me before.'

He spoke softly, 'But I bin thinkin' 'bout you a long, long time.'

Colour flooded her face. When it drained away, she had the dreadful faint feeling again.

'But how could you?' she whispered again, and

wanted to lean forward, put her head on his shoulder and feel his arms go around her.

'Little kids think about bein' grow'd up and merried. I did – lots. Cuz I didn't have no folks. . . .'

'Oh – were you an orphan?'

'Dunno, mebbe. Mebbe jess lost. I useter think that somewhere in the world *right now* they wuz that girl – *her* that would belong to me some day. Then I'd have folks. An' I knew I'd recognize her the moment I laid eyes on her.'

She said nothing. It was quite a long time before she even looked up at him. Then she saw the question in his eyes. He was asking her. Would she? Was she? And within herself she was answering, Oh, yes! Yes! But it had already happened. She was committed. Out loud she said, 'What's your name?'

He said, 'Joey.'

She looked down at the ground at her right side and said, smiling, 'Joey.'

He leaned over the fence, 'Say it again! Oh, call me that again as eff'n you recognized me too.'

'I didn't call you that. I just said it.'

'Say it again.' But she would not.

'Are you going to be working here?'

'Yup. I'm to start on the hay crew tomorrer.'

'Oh. And what today?'

'Jess settle in. Get to know the ranch. My quarters is above the tack room in the horse stable.'

'Did they tell you anything else?'

'Tole me to put my pony in the big pasture above the horse stable. I wuz jess goin to do that wen you come out.'

'Do you know the way?'

'I ain't never been up thar but I guess I cud find it.'

'I'll show you the way,' said Letty and took a step toward the fence. Joey had seen how easily she

28

could climb it but now he reached over as if to lift her.

'Kin I help you over?'

Letty stopped and backed away. 'Thank you. I'll go around by the gate.'

In a moment she was at his side, no fence between them. They had never been so close to each other before. On each face there dawned the faintest smile, hardly more than a parting of the lips; but the eyes, meeting, clinging, probing, held them together with hypnotic power. Letty could not endure it. She turned her head, looked down and tried to make her voice steady.

'You can bring your pony around by the gate.'

They went single file, Letty leading the way, then Joey with his horse at his shoulder.

A sudden gust of wind hit them and Letty had to hold her skirt to keep it from whirling around her. The narrow path led across the large clearing. Letty named the buildings as they came to them, calling over her shoulder.

'That's the spring house. And here, on this side, this is the bunkhouse.'

The path went between the two buildings then there were hillocks on each side of it making it just a narrow defile, winding crookedly to higher ground.

Then it widened, opened up and there was another clearing in which was a big horse stable. There was an upper storey over the tack room with gables and windows, and around one side a series of corrals. The fences were high with closely placed rails. Letty explained that here was where the wild broncs were brought to be broken and trained.

She spoke mechanically as if hardly knowing what she was saying. She glanced at the sky and the scudding clouds. 'If it storms today – and it looks like it, they'll cover up the hay that's already been cut with tarps and come back here. Poppa will be grim. If it's just a shower they'll stay in the field.'

They entered the largest corral and Joey unsaddled Roy. The opposite gate opened on to a wide pasture.

Holding saddle and bridle on his left arm and his hat in his right hand, Joey whacked Roy on the haunches with the hat and yelled, 'Yippee!'

The pony galloped through the open gate, out into the wide pasture, then expressed his pleasure. He stopped, looked all around him with pricked ears, then gave several wild whinneys, then he bucked for the pure joy of it. Finally he threw himself down and rolled. When he got to his feet he shook himself hard and with one last flirt of his heels galloped off around a wooded shoulder.

Letty stood waiting while Joey carried his accoutrements into the tack room. When he emerged his hat was in his hand. He held it by the brim, squinted at one of the corral posts, aimed carefully, then sent the hat spinning through the air. It made a gentle curve, sank, then settled on the post, swirling a little before coming to rest.

'Oh! You're good with a lasso,' said Letty.

'Kin use a rope.'

Joey walked to the open gate and pointed in the direction the pony had taken.

'Wot's around there?' he asked.

Letty moved to his side. 'Just more pastures,' she said.

'Cud we take a little walk now we're up here?'

Letty walked beside him as one in a dream. Their hands, swinging between them, touched by accident. Immediately Joey's hand turned and clasped hers. Now they walked hand in hand.

Suddenly the sky darkened. Joey looked up.

'Reckon we gonna git wet.'

Huge drops spattered around them. Joey cried, 'In them woods where the pony went,' and they started to run but the rain was upon them.

'The aspen grove!' shrieked Letty. 'It's nearer.' They swerved to the left.

The trees were good shelter but it was a deluge and they were drenched when they got there. Joey's arm was around her. They faced each other, laughing. Joey hugged her. It was not an embrace, it was just a hug. She was wiping the rain from her cheeks and pushing her wet hair back. Their faces touched – pressed together and Letty felt soft kisses on her forehead and eyelids. Then it was no longer a hug, it was an embrace and they stopped laughing. He was holding her closely and tenderly.

Letty had never been kissed except in kissing games in childhood, but she had often thought of it. How sweet it would be if it was the right man! And how horrible and unpleasant if it was not.

Holding her close to him with one arm, Joey brought his other hand up to take hold of her chin and gently turn her face so that their lips came together. Then again he wrapped both arms around her. They held each other as if they would never let each other go. Their mouths clung together and the two young bodies intertwined.

The shower ended as quickly as it had begun, the sun came out and a rainbow spanned the sky.

Down on the hayfield they put the tarps away and continued with the work.

Chapter Six

Now the sun was blazing. The two young people sat on a big fallen log near the corral and dried out.

Joey said, 'We gonna git married now, Letty?'

'Of course, Joey.'

But the question was really superfluous. Had they not plighted their troth that morning at sunrise in a meeting of eyes that was like a marriage?

They embraced again. Could not let go of each other.

Joey said, 'I never knowed a feller could be so happy.'

They remained in this private world of their own. Looks, smiles, caresses, murmurs.

They had a great deal to say to each other. They must continue the talk that had begun when they stood with the fence between them. Much more than that, there was the earlier meeting when she was at her window and he below on his horse – all this was pent up within them.

Suddenly Letty said, 'You know – your eyes simply held me. I couldn't look away.'

And Joey answered, 'Neither cud I.'

Then they relived all the memories of the last few hours, moment by moment. It had brought them to this peace, to each other, freedom from everything else.

'Joey,' said Letty, ' you told me that you were a lost boy. How old were you when you got lost?'

'Dunno, Letty. Too little to remember anything about it.'

'Tell me the very earliest thing you can remember.'

'That dawg, a yaller dawg. His name wuz Yaller.'

He told her about the dog he had slept on the floor with, hugged up close. And chased chickens with in the daytime.

'But who taught you your name? Joey – that sounds like a pet name. It stands for Joseph, you know.'

'I reckon a little kid larns his name like a puppy. Here, Joey – here, Joey – And that's as soon as he can walk. I *allers* wuz Joey.'

Letty laughed, looking up at the sun. He kissed her and they stopped talking for a while. Then she said, 'But what about your second name? Your family name, Bud?'

The face she had been looking at, a boy's face, warm and beautiful, happy and living and open, now changed completely. It became a poker face and a man's face.

It was a story Joey had to tell often. He never flinched from it. And he told it again in practically the same words with which he had related it to Jim Billings.

Letty listened at first astonished then unbelieving. 'Why Joey, if this is true – if you don't know who you really are, then your whole family tree is lost.'

'A tree?'

'Your ancestors. Your parents' parents all the way back to Adam. Maybe poets and kings and geniuses. They're all part of you. And the name would be a fix on them. There would be some way – your parents would have tied a little chain around your neck, with a locket on it, or they'd have put some mark on you. . . .'

Joey laughed and looked like a boy again. 'You mean a brand like we put on the foals and calves?'

'Of course, then if your parents found you, they'd know who you were.'

'Aw Letty – they ain't a-lookin' for me. Not after all these years. They've forgot about it, like I hev. It's too long ago.'

'Oh, no, Joey. Parents never stop looking for their lost children. Like Windy.'

'Windy? Who's Windy?'

'An old fellow that visits at our sheep camp. He's lost his grandson and he goes around asking everyone, "Have you seen my little lost boy?"'

'Sounds cracked.'

'He is. But it's really true. His grandson is lost. Unless it's you, Joey. That would fit nicely. Then he'd have his grandson and you'd have a grandfather and a real name.'

It was said as a joke, a crazy idea, but the moment she had said it Letty realized it was not impossible at all, it could be true. And she tried to remember all the things she had heard about Windy, things everybody knew. He had once, long ago, been a lecturer at Harvard and his real name was something-or-other Willoughby, an important-sounding, even distinguished name.

She tried to calculate the years. 'Joey, how old are you? But, there's no way you can know that?'

'Yes, I know. I'm twenty, jess the right age fer you.'

'I'm eighteen.'

A rapturous smile and kiss sealed this testimony.

'But Joey, how can you know?'

'Cuz, wen Mr Untermeyer's bull gored me, I wuz eight and—'

Letty gave a little scream, but Joey made nothing of it.

'When Mr Untermeyer cum to the hospital to get me and pay the bill he ast the doc how old he thought I wuz

34

because I wuz tall, and Doc looked at my teeth – same as you'd do with a hoss and said eight years old. Add twelve to eight an' that makes twenty.'

There was another pause given over to nothing but bliss.

'Yes, but Joey, that figure. Twelve. Where did you get that? Just a guess?'

'Nope. I didn't know the day wen I was eight, but I knowed it was hayin' time. Every year, hayin' time, I knowed I wuz a year older. Right up till now.'

'That's pretty good figuring.'

'I c'd allers count. Quarter an apple an' you got four pieces. Split each an' you got eight. Take away three an' you got five.' Joey finished, 'Figurin' and countin' is easy.'

'Readin' is easy too,' Joey said. 'Someone jess shows me a word and tells me wot it means, then I've got it.'

'Don't you forget it?'

'I nivver forgits,' Joey answered simply.

'But Joey, who showed it to you the first time? That was a teacher?'

'Nope. It war that little ole Granny.'

'Whose Granny? Tell me about her.'

'I hired out at a big ranch jess to do chores fer my keep. Figured I'd be trampin' through snow all winter carryin' swill to the pigs and choppin' wood. But they put me in a big warm room to take keer of that Granny. She was lame, sat in a chair, needed someone to fetch an carry for her and stoke the stove. I wuz ten. I could do that. But I guess she was a kind of teacher.

'She taught me lots. She taught me about men; how you could tell a bad one by the smell of his sweat. How you could tell one you must obey by the ring in his voice. How I must be proud and hold my head up no matter wot I was. Depend on myself. Nobuddy else would do it for me. "Do your work well. Do it with a

35

will. Learn everything there is to do on a ranch and you'll never go hungry." But mostly she didn't talk, jess sat in that cheer an I stoked the stove and kep her warm. That was my job. I knowed she had tuk a shine to me. One day her hands were cold. I held them and rubbed them but they got colder and colder.

'She said, "Pull me nearer the stove," and I did, pulled her chair close. She leaned her head back and closed her eyes and I kept rubbin' her hands.'

Joey was silent for a while, then said, 'But her hands nivver got warm again. I left that place.'

The sun went under a cloud and suddenly they were in shadow, then it blazed out again and the wind blew a fold of Letty's skirt across his leg.

He said, 'Gittin' dry, honey?' He felt her skirt. 'Pretty damp still.' Then he carefully rearranged the skirt over his knee where the wind had blown it.

Such intimacy! They smiled into each other's eyes, then Letty hid her face against him. But there was much more she wanted to know.

'Joey, what was the very first real home you had? Some place where they took care of you and were good to you?'

'Aw, Letty, they wuz all good to me. Everbuddy will take keer of a little kid. He kin allers do chores.'

'What chores?'

'Milk. I wuz a good milker. I wuz milkin' fer Mr Untermeyer when his bull gored me.'

'Didn't it make a difference to people that you were a lost boy and didn't know who your parents were.'

'To some it did. A feller at a dance tole me to quit dancin' with his sister, he got me by the shoulder. He wuz a lot bigger'n me.'

Letty was horrified. 'What did you do?'

'I quit. Didn't want to be put off the floor.'

'But didn't you *care*?'

36

As remembrance came to Joey, Letty saw his face change, become older, expressionless, poker-faced. Where had his radiant, boyish happiness gone?

'I keered, Letty. But if they's somethin' you want but you can't get you aren't goin' to cry about it are you?'

Letty did not answer. She could not. She was near tears herself. He had come through all this with no trace of bitterness or self-pity; with gratitude in his heart for those who had helped him, gaiety and high spirits.

Joey went to retrieve his hat. Letty got up from the log and stood thinking deeply. Joey had said he was twenty. She calculated the age of Windy's Grandson. It must be just about the same. And as Joey returned to her she exclaimed, her face alight, 'Why Joey! You and Windy's lost grandson must be almost exactly the same age!'

'Aw, Letty, they ain't no one standin' in my boots but me, Joey Bud.'

Letty's face sobered. She looked at him without answering. He was disturbed.

'Letty, about my name – *Bud* – is it all right with you?'

'Well, no, Joey. Of course it isn't your real name. It's a mask. A disguise. It simply covers you up.'

'But Letty, wen we're married it'll be your name too.'

Letty was silent but her whole attitude repudiated such a possibility.

Joey cried, 'It's the only name I got any sorta right to. Wen we're married you don't want to be Mrs BUD?'

She shook her head.

'How dumb I bin,' he cried, his voice hard and his face blank.

'Oh, Joey!' She flung her arms around him. 'Don't look like that. It doesn't matter! What's good enough for you is good enough for me!'

He put his hand on her chest and gently pushed her off a little so that he could look into her eyes. 'Sure, Letty?'

'Yes, Joey, I'm sure.'

As if they were reunited after a long separation they held each other with a new passion – with laughter too. How silly to have imagined that they could be separated by a name, by anything.

It was two o'clock. The harsh vertical rays of noon had moved. Now they slanted down, edging every line with a delicate frill of shadow. But the sun was still blazing, pouring out floods of golden light.

It was time to go back. They walked slowly down the long twisted path until they reached the clearing. There they stood facing each other to say good-bye. It was only a temporary parting but hard.

Down in the hayfield there had been trouble with one of the broncs. Wagon and harness had been kicked to pieces. They could repair the wagon on the spot but the harness was ruined, and Hank and Swede had driven back to the shop to get another.

Of all the stone and log buildings that encircled the clearing, the shop was on the highest ground with considerable cleared land around it and a service road sweeping off and around to enter the meadow.

While Hank rummaged in the shop for what he wanted Swede turned the car around then brought it to the door of the shop and stopped it.

Hank came out of the shop with the harness but before he got into the car, happened to look down and saw Letty and Joey standing there, saying good-bye. He halted and stood a few moments staring.

It was true that Hank wanted no man on the ranch

who could rival him in good looks. He counted his compliments like a girl. In college he had been teased about being just the type fortune tellers promise – 'A tall dark man will come into your life.'

Hank was tall although perhaps too heavy, but his erect posture and over-bearing manner counterbalanced that. His hair and eyes were dark and he was undeniably handsome.

Women admired him. The one he wanted was Letty Heath and he had earmarked her for himself. His girl.

'Look at that,' Hank said.

Swede was already looking and with considerable surprise. He was looking down at the clearing where Joey and Letty stood facing each other near the door of her house, saying good-bye.

'Why, for Pete's sake,' Swede exclaimed. 'They look as if they wuz old friends. Did they know each other before he cum here today?'

'I hired him this morning,' Hank said. 'The Boss wished him on me. The son of a b---.'

He got into the car and Swede started it.

Chapter Seven

When Letty went to bed that night she could not sleep. The events of the day had filled her veins with a potent stimulant. She felt as if she would never sleep again. It was true then. There was a power that could seize and hold you, lift you to heights you had never dreamed of. Change everything.

Mixed with the joy and excitement was a recurrent anxiety, about the matter of breaking the news of her engagement to her parents. She knew it had to be done, and soon. But parents so often made difficulties, especially fathers.

Marriage was natural and inevitable. They wouldn't want their daughter to be an old maid. But so often, when the time came, they were unwilling, even when it was an ordinary engagement, proper and conventional with nothing wrong about the name.

Parents. You said the word as if it meant just one person. They were *one* as a wedded couple, of course, sleeping in the same bed and having only one name between them. But to her, their child, they were definitely two persons, and very different. Almost opposite. She would not mind telling her mother. Their relationship was that of comrades. She knew she'd get as much understanding as if it was someone of her own age she was confiding in.

As a matter of fact, there was a quality of agelessness about Martha Heath. She was as tall and slender as Letty, as quick and agile. She could not be called a beauty but her face was charming and expressive. There was as yet no grey in her thick, dark hair which she wore pushed up and around her head leaving her lovely forehead bare. Her eyes were dark and laughing. It would be a great relief to pour it all out to her.

But to her father? Her thoughts recoiled. She would dread that. She couldn't do it. She *wouldn't* do it. She would delegate that to her mother.

Few people go through life without experiencing, at least a few times, a white night as it is called. When there is no such thing as sleep or sleepiness, as if they were rapt away from this world where such things are normal, and taken somewhere where no such thing exists.

Letty's eyes did not close. The hours passed. She was, more than awake, infused with the fiery essence that enables one to reach impossible heights. It lasted until dawn when, with the suddenness of a fall, she sank into unconsciousness.

A couple of hours later she awoke and had no recollection of all that had happened. Her mind was empty, a clean slate.

She stretched and yawned. Then came the intimation, vague at first, of *something*, something important, something wonderful. Oh, what was it? What was it? Full recollection struck her like a blow and she leaped out of bed. Joey! Oh, Joey!

She stood a few moments in a daze of bliss, deeply excited, aware of an immense alteration in her life. She was different. Everything was different.

She sat down on the edge of her bed and gave herself to the remembering of all that had happened.

Nothing would ever be the same again. And this was no experience of her own imagining, no dream or wishful vision, but a fact.

The realization ebbed, then came again. Again and again, great slow waves pounding on her, and the beginning of it so simple a thing as her casual glance downward. Into the eyes of Joey.

Letty's downward glance was pure accident. Its power to alter, to transmute, was the same, but it brought her nothing but wonder and joy.

Joey, meanwhile, and others of the hay crew, worked under the commanding eye of Jepson Heath out-doing themselves in a desperate effort to get the whole crop in before the weather turned.

Jepson knew the risks as well as the possible rewards. He had seen a flash flood turn a meadow into a lake in a single hour. He had seen electric storms turn the whole sky into a sheet of white fire, blinking on and off and sending balls of flame running along the barbed wire fences. And he had seen the opposite. Ice storms, dropping hail that was at first the size of marbles, then ping pong balls then tennis balls, at last chunks of ice big enough to kill a sheep. In Wyoming the weather could behave like a mortal enemy.

Bad weather was brewing now, Jepson could see it. A ring of purplish clouds just below the horizon, pushing up now and then showing their dark snouts, then retreating. If they could get the hay in before those clouds rose up and advanced across the sky, all would be well.

He worked in the field as hard as any of them. His vigilant eye was everywhere, on men and horses, watchful to forestall trouble or prevent delay.

And there was always the possibility of accidents. Farming, hay-making was dangerous business. Machinery was dangerous. And they had only one really experienced and reliable work team, old Nellie and Prince. The rest were half broken broncs, strong to work and pull but liable to go berserk at any moment. Then anything could happen.

Martha turned all household duties over to Letty and held herself ready at a moment's notice in case she had to drive an injured man in the Studebaker to the nearest doctor. Or, if it was a horse, the trip would be to the Cottonwood Post Office where there was a telephone to call the veterinarian. Or perhaps just to drive to Laramie to fetch some small but indispensable machine part.

A day passed and Letty had not even caught a glimpse of Joey. Nor had she been able to talk to her mother.

Another day passed.

Chapter Eight

'Oh, Momma, please stop doing that. I've something to tell you.'

'Well, go right on, child, you know I've got to make out my list.'

'But it's important, Momma! *Please* listen.'

'I *am* listening. *Flour, coffee, tobacco*. What's so important?'

'I want to tell you about Joey Bud.'

Martha was seated at her desk and Letty was curled up in a big armchair talking to her mother's back.

Martha said, 'There's nobody on the ranch of that name unless it's one of the new fellows.'

'He *is* one of the new fellows.'

'But what difference can he make to you? One more hired hand. You've seen dozens of them. They come and go. Letty, didn't you tell me you had some books to go back to the library? If you'll bring them to me ...' She wrote on her list, *Books to library*.

Letty said, 'But this particular hired hand *does* make a difference to me. A lot ...'

Martha became motionless, then lifted her head.

Letty continued, 'Now perhaps you'll let me tell you what happened.'

'Happened?'

'The other morning. Early.'

Martha laid down her pencil and turned to face her daughter. 'Happened! What *could* happen?'

'Well, Momma, when I woke up I could see that it

was early because the sun was just rising. A gorgeous sunrise. The colours poured into my room – pink and red . . .'

'Your windows standing open of course?'

Letty's windows were casement windows, open vertically in the centre.

'They always are,' said Letty. 'I got up and went to the window to look at the sunrise. Then I looked down. There was a man down there, on a horse, staring up at me.'

'Great heavens!' exclaimed Martha. 'Were you dressed?'

'Not exactly. Just my nightgown.'

'You shouldn't have let him see you in your nightgown.'

'I know. But what could I do? There I was. And there he was.'

'You should have left the window.'

'Of course. I did. It was just a few seconds.'

'How many seconds?'

'Oh, Momma! How can I tell? Ten. Or fifteen. Or twenty.'

Martha was silent, thinking of all the things that can happen in a few seconds. A lightning flash. Perhaps to illumine, perhaps strike dead. A decision made, perhaps fortunate, perhaps the first fatal step on a downward, one-way path – never to be reversed.

'That's when it happened,' interrupted Letty.

'For the land's sake! He didn't speak to you?'

'Oh, no, Momma. It was a look we gave each other. At first it was accidental. Our eyes just happened to meet. But then they held. We couldn't look away. We were simply locked together.'

'That isn't a nice way to talk!' chided Martha gently, 'But I suppose you were terribly frightened?'

'No, Momma, I wasn't. I just . . .'

45

'Well, what?'

'I fell in love with him.'

'Letty Heath!'

'Why, Momma! You sound shocked.'

'I am!'

'But why? Isn't love good? Isn't it just wonderful?'

'Oh, Letty, a girl can't understand these things.'

'A girl can *feel*. . . . I did. It's all true.'

'But *so fast* – Everything happening in a flash like that and then you taking it so seriously.'

'Isn't there such a thing as love at first sight?' And Letty drew a deep sobbing sigh.

Martha looked at her daughter almost in alarm, then asked, gently, 'Was it really like that, child? At the first sight?'

'Well – by the time that look ended it was love – I kind of . . . went out to him you know.'

'Mercy me—' murmured Martha and then was silent.

'Momma, I've got lots more to tell you.'

Martha gave a little moan and abandoned all idea of going to Laramie that afternoon. She put away her pencils and lists and swung her chair around. 'But first, Letty, what about Hank?'

'Hank?' repeated Letty as if it was an unfamiliar name.

'Yes, Hank. Aren't you, in a way, engaged to him?'

'Certainly not.'

'He is devoted to you. And you've encouraged him?'

'Never.'

'Letty, I think you must have. When you're out together, don't you let him kiss you?'

'I do not.' At her mother's inquiring and somewhat doubting look, Letty said, 'He tried it once, but never again. Just that once.'

Martha's eyebrows went up. 'By force, you mean?'

'Yes.'

'What did you do?'

'Kicked and bit and clawed, tore loose and ran away while he was mopping up the blood.'

'For Heaven's sake!' But Martha did not seem too astonished. She went on, 'Then I'm sure he was sorry and begged you to forgive him. And you did?'

'Oh, in a way, but I never trusted him again.'

'But, Letty, you went out with him in his car, to parties, I mean.'

'Never alone. I'd have Blossom in the back seat.'

'Not Blossom!' exclaimed Martha.

Blossom was a fat old Indian woman, a retainer of the Heath family from way back. She was a sight to behold, dressed in overalls she made herself out of gunny sacks. A perpetual grin showed she only had a few teeth. But she could do anything that needed doing and was as faithful as old Nellie.

Letty was laughing. 'It made Hank so mad he wouldn't speak.'

'I don't blame him,' said Martha.

'But, Momma, why are you kind of standing up for Hank?'

'He's a splendid fellow and we've known him a long time. He's devoted to you, and you – well, so far, you've only made a sort of convenience of him. But that sort of relationship can turn into something quite different if you'll only give it time. So I advise you . . .'

Letty interrupted, 'But, Momma, how can you talk that way, as if I still had a choice, when I've told you about Joey Bud, and what has already happened between him and me?'

Martha sighed. 'So it's Joey Bud. I can't say I care for the name.'

'*Bud* isn't his real name. Not his parents' name. Not a family name. He just uses it.'

47

'For Heaven's sake! An assumed name! Why in the world would he do a thing like that? I don't like it, Letty. It looks bad. As if he was concealing something disgraceful.'

'I know,' said Letty. 'It *is* bad. It's awful. But it's nothing disgraceful and it's not Joey's fault. You see, he's a lost boy.'

'A lost boy?'

'Lost when he was too young to remember anything about it, even his parents' name.'

Then Letty outlined to her mother the events of Joey's childhood as he had related them to her.

Martha listened, interested, astonished, sometimes perturbed, sometimes doubting. When it was finished, she sat thinking it over in silence.

Letty added regretfully, 'Of course, it's too bad that the first person Joey can remember is a dog.'

Martha made no reply to that.

'Isn't it pathetic, Momma? A childhood like that? Brought up by strangers?' said Letty.

'Pathetic? Well, I don't know. Kind, friendly people around him. Food and shelter. He could have fared worse.'

'Now, Momma, I've got some more ...'

Martha threw up her hands, 'No more, Letty! Please! No more shocks!'

'This isn't a shock, Momma. This is good.'

'I can hardly believe it.'

'This is the answer to everything.'

'Heavens! Let's have it.'

'Momma, what other lost boy did you ever hear about? Lost in this part of the country?'

'None. Never heard of such a thing. No lost boys. Except, of course, old Windy's.'

'Well, there you are.'

'What do you mean?'

48

'It's so obvious. I guessed at once. Joey is the grandson Windy has been hunting for all these years.'

'But it's a *little* boy Windy's searching for.'

'He *was* a little boy, fifteen years ago. And so was Joey!'

Martha's face lit up. Her mouth fell open. 'Well, I declare! Right under our noses. However did you manage to ferret it out?'

'Ferret it out?' repeated Letty.

'Yes. What link did you find to tie the two together – Windy's lost grandson and this other lost boy, Joey what's-his-name?'

'It just came to me in a flash. And once you've thought of it, it's so obvious you don't see how anyone could miss it.'

'I don't know about that. It *could* be true, of course, but I would call it a very slim chance – not what you could call proof at all.'

'But, Momma, what else could it be?'

'He could be lost on purpose by an unwed mother just to get rid of him. A foundling. And you know what that means.'

Indeed Letty did know, for the newspapers had been full of the story. The little box, not much bigger than a shoe box, found under a bench in the station. And in the box, a newborn baby.

Letty's eyes were horrorstruck. She exclaimed passionately, 'You only have to look at Joey to know he's not one of those.'

'Appearance has nothing to do with it. Think of all the catch colts! Foals that are dropped on these plains where there are so many bands of wild horses running loose. Handsome, many of them, and perhaps with the finest Arabian blood in them, but no known sire to give them a name and certify the blood line. For that you

49

must have registration papers. Your Joey, I presume, has no papers.'

'Oh, Momma—'

'Every cow in our herd is a pure-bred Guernsey and her papers prove it.'

'But you don't register human beings.'

'You certainly do. A marriage licence is a paper, isn't it? And when the baby comes, a birth certificate. Isn't that a paper? Letty, we'd like to feel as sure of our grandchildren and great-grandchildren as we do of our cows.'

'But if he is Windy's grandson . . .'

'If. . . . *If*. That's a very big *if*.'

'But Momma, you said that it might be true. It *could* be true. There is a chance that it is.'

'Yes, a chance. And that's all.'

'Momma, if it was you? If you had fallen in love with someone the way I've fallen in love with Joey, wouldn't you take that chance?'

'Oh, Letty . . .' Martha stalled.

'Wouldn't you, Momma?'

'Letty, perhaps I would have. When I was your age. And even now, perhaps I'd give in to you, proof or no proof. But it's not only me, it's your father too. And he would never consent unless you had proof.'

'But, Momma, you could talk to him and explain it to him and persuade him.'

'Bother him about something like this when he's already so worried about the haying? I wouldn't think of it!'

'Then after haying,' pleaded Letty.

'Oh, Letty. A man with no name! No folks! No home! No background! No, I can't think this would be right.'

Letty whispered, 'Oh, Momma, won't you help me?' And her face was stricken.

Martha took her daughter's hand and held it lovingly. 'Letty – just put all this out of your head – just go back these few days. You can, I'm sure, dearie – you can get over it.'

Letty did not answer at all. She looked at her mother and the tears overflowed.

Martha said weakly, 'Don't cry, child. Well . . . then . . . after haying . . . I'll see what I can do.'

Chapter Nine

Then, having given her promise to Letty, Martha didn't have a moment's peace of mind. How could she have committed herself when she didn't know the man? This Joey Bud. She had seen him, of course, and noticed his good looks but hadn't given him a second thought. Why, he might be a scheming imposter!

This reaction hit her almost as soon as Letty was out of sight, and with it the realization that she had to do something about it immediately. Get to know him. Get a real understanding of him so that she would be able to weigh his worth. Not merely a brief inspection.

Before she went to bed she sent Blossom to the bunkhouse with a message for Hank telling him that when she went to Laramie next morning she would bring back the heavy things that were needed, grain, cement and so forth. He should please attach the two-wheeled trailer to the Studebaker. One man should accompany her. Joey Bud.

And not for anything must any worry about this be added to her husband's worries about the hay. She would keep it to herself. He would be down in the field working, long before she left in the morning. He would be watching the sky, the weather, worrying about that hard shower the other day.

He lay beside her now in the big walnut bed, sleeping like a log after the day's exertions. She lay on her pillow, he on his, the light in the room was very dim. But by a slight turn of her head she could see his craggy shape, one big shoulder thrust up, his handsome head outlined against the pillow by the thick flat curls which hugged his scalp.

She wondered why she should feel so protective towards this stalwart man made of stone because he had so much more than physical power. Inner strength. Also a touch of mystery hinted at by his dark eyes which she could not quite fathom.

She turned and moved carefully towards him, inch by inch, not wanting to wake him. She caught the faint scent of a soap which he used. Of course, he had showered before coming to bed, as he always did. The bed creaked. She stopped moving and lay quite still but both his arms reached out and gathered her to him, cradling her comfortably against his body.

It was an accustomed procedure and did not wake him. Her cheek rested on his shoulder. His breath bathed her forehead. It was sweet. It smelled like a cow's breath.

At last she slept.

As she got ready to go next morning, she realized that she was a little tense. It was going to be an encounter and she was gathering her forces. In spite of her determination to be objective, she felt like a prosecuting attorney. There ought to be a lawyer for the defence too, she thought. Hardly fair to expect an ignorant hired hand to plead his own case.

As she walked towards the Studebaker the first thing that caught her notice was how clean the car looked, the trailer too. The tall young fellow who stood holding the door open for her had the same spick and span appearance.

'Mornin', Ma'am,' he said pleasantly.

'Good morning,' she answered stiffly and got into

the car. He closed the door and walked around the front to take the wheel.

As he went, Martha studied him carefully. He moved well, held himself well. Sometimes it was perfect proportions that gave a man that kind of grace. Sometimes it was a quality of their personality. Inborn.

This observation increased her feeling of antagonism. What chance did her child have against anyone so smooth? That's what he was – smooth.

Joey, mindful of the trailer, was paying attention to his driving, the turn at the bottom of the incline then the second turn that swung them out on to the meadow road.

Martha struggled to hold her emotions in check because she had to think clearly. This day must produce results. She was going to question him exhaustively. She had to know everything about him that he could be made to tell her. And she would not try to be tactful. If he got huffy, or evasive, that would be so many counts against him. It was the feel of the man she wanted to get. After a day spent with him she would know if he was fit to be Letty's husband or not. He was bound to give himself away sooner or later.

As they crossed the meadow she said, 'Do you do this kind of thing often, Joey Bud?'

He was silent for so long that she explained further, 'I mean, take any girl you want? Practically at first sight?'

Joey Bud's habitual expression of good temper changed under Martha's attack. He realized that they were antagonists and put on his armour.

He was no less polite, and spoke slowly and carefully, 'No, Ma'am. I ain't never taken girls thataways. Not any. Not for keeps, that is. Not till Letty.'

'Not till Letty!' repeated Martha angrily. The

words stung. But what was the use? It was the brutal truth.

Then he turned to look at her. She met his gaze. There in the car for a few seconds they measured each other.

He said, 'Me and Letty,' and stopped, then looked back at the road as if there was nothing more to be said.

Presently she began her interrogation. Her questions were searching and intimate but not unfriendly and he neither evaded nor showed resentment. As if he admitted her right, he answered, but offered nothing extra, did not hold forth about himself, did not actually speak unless he was spoken to.

So she learned about all the ranches he had lived at. About the dog and the bull and the old Granny. About the horses he had broken. She took special notice of his efforts to get the know-how of everything he did and the pride it aroused in him when he found he could do a man's work and support himself.

His physical qualifications were apparent. The handsomeness of his head and face kept her looking at him, in fact, made it impossible for her not to. As for points such as a livestock breeder would notice, she knew the extreme height and slenderness often denoted weakness and awkwardness, but in Joey's case every motion he made was well controlled and economical. He used just as much strength as was needed, and his supply of it, seemingly, was unlimited. At the elevator he lifted the hundred-pound sacks of grain to his shoulder effortlessly, something which even Hank did not do. He manoeuvred the car and trailer through the streets of Laramie without difficulty, and this was not easy. The skill and care he showed in all he had to do attested to a high degree of 'know-how'.

When the errands were done they sat in the car and ate the lunch Blossom had put up for them. On the ride

55

home there was little talk. Martha's anger had melted away. She had got the feel of him and was summing up.

He was quite mature in some ways – his abilities, his self-possession, and particularly his concept of himself. He expected a great deal from himself and took it for granted that others would too. But how young he was, how childlike – those flat, blunt answers, just the sort of answers a child would give. Honest? Of course, not old enough to be devious. Not smart enough. Yes, it was innocence. Not like Letty's simple natural innocence which was like the bloom of a peach, but all the same . . .

Well – they were both children. And what a power it gave them!

Many miles passed. They were nearing the ranch.

The verdict was in, at last, and Martha whispered it to herself. 'He's quite a man.'

He only lacked the one all-important thing, a father's name. And Letty had made herself believe that he had that too.

Well, perhaps it was true.

It was not until they had got home and were parting that Joey finished the sentence he had begun that morning.

'Me and Letty,' he said simply, 'we aims to git married.'

'So I gather,' said Martha drily. And they looked at each other as if there was nothing more to be said, but Martha added, 'It's rather sudden you must admit. What you've got to do now is get to know each other. Why, you're hardly acquainted yet.'

'Wa-al—' began Joey argumentatively, for it seemed to him that much of his life had passed since his first glimpse of Letty.

But Martha cut him short with a brief good-night and the door of her house closed between them.

She stood inside a moment thinking about the amazing part chance plays in life for it was nothing but chance that had brought about that long look between Letty and Joey. If she had not happened to look down! If he had not been just there!

But having looked and held on and joined in the looking was not chance at all. They had fallen in love with each other.

Chapter Ten

As if to cancel out all memories of storms and floods and ice, good weather for haying on the Heath Ranch was no less than heavenly. It was idyllic.

Men, horses and machines moved down the half-mile-long hay meadows as if all had been arranged by a great choreographer. The pace was controlled, the rhythm maintained and the team work expertly coordinated.

The mowing machines went first through the rippling green sea of grass. It was so high it brushed the eyes of the horses. The drivers held them with difficulty to a sedate pace – slow, regular steps down the meadow leaving a thick flat carpet behind.

The rakes followed, drawn by horses that trotted, moving lightly, swinging this way and that, gathering the fallen grass into long windrows. From the new-mown hay rose a delicious fragrance which perfumed the air for scores of miles.

The whirrings of the mowing machines and the shouts of the men rang with the strange and faintly sad hollowness characteristic of sounds heard in the open from a distance.

Joining the chorus was the occasional lonely cry of a hawk as he hung high over the field, watching. His wings were stretched to their fullest but did not move. He rode the air currents tilting a little, gliding away, circling back, with effortless mastery. But this was not pleasurable idling, he was hunting. The long swathes of falling grass disclosed tiny living things at their roots. Field mice or moles, little snakes, gophers, these were his prey.

A jarring note in the summer idyll was the tension between Hank Burrows and Joey Bud. They felt it to a man, knew that there would be trouble sooner or later, and were on the lookout for it.

It came, sparked by a trifle, almost a ludicrous trifle, as so often happens.

It was late in the afternoon and they were taking wagon loads of hay out of the field. Swede, driving one of these wagons and having trouble with his team, called to Joey for help. One horse was plunging, standing on its hind legs.

Joey went to the head of the team and brought the unmanageable bronco down on all fours. While he examined the bit, a sudden gust of wind lifted his hat from his head, carried it off and dropped it. Joey laughed but continued working with the bit. The hat behaved as hats often do. It lay still, then made several hops, then crawled a few feet. An eddy of wind now turned it upside down, then flopped it over again. Several of the men were watching and grinning when Hank tossed a load of hay on to the wagon, pulled loose his pitchfork, drove it into the ground and leaped for Joey's hat. He stamped on it yelling with laughter and smashed the crown flat.

It was not the first time that Joey had remembered and obeyed the old Granny's teaching, 'When you've got to fight, Joey, and there'll be plenty of times – hit him first. A good lick.' Joey hit him now, a good lick but not a fist blow, it was a tackle and they both went down, Joey on top. He was up in a flash and turned his back on Hank to retrieve his battered hat. That gave Hank his chance. In a slow fury he rose, took his pitchfork and aimed.

A blow like a sledge hammer fell on his shoulder, Jepson roared, 'Now stop this nonsense, boys! You, Joey, get on the rake! Hank, take your team!' And the work began again.

For this episode Jepson Heath chose to punish Joey.

He banished him from the hay crew and sent him to work in the Pine Grove where, on the first of September, Old Timers' picnic would be held.

Joey was to dig the barbecue pits where, on the great day, sides of beef would be roasted. He was to dig post holes where the dance pavilion would be set up; dig to level a square where a waxed canvas would be laid for dancing. He was to dig out old tree stumps. He was to dig.

He whistled as he worked. He knew that in the noon hour Letty would be there beside him carrying a small picnic basket with lunch for two.

The fight was endlessly discussed in the bunkhouse.

Gilly, the Irish wrangler, said, 'I don't get it. Hank started it but the Boss takes it out on Joey. Sends him way up there to the pine grove to work all alone.'

Swede said, 'You can't blame Hank. Not if he'd speared him. Joey took his girl.'

'Letty has never been Hank's girl,' said Jim Billings.

They all spoke at once. She was, and she wasn't.

But Jim insisted, 'She never really fell for Hank.'

'And she's sure stuck on Joey – the way she looks at him—' said Sid.

Swede said, 'Emily Haskell told me that Hank told her that he and Letty are secretly engaged.'

'But she's got a right to choose,' said Gilly.

Sid agreed. 'And if it's Joey she chooses ...'

Swede's voice rose, 'But who's Joey? He don't know himself! That makes him a catch colt, don't it?'

'The Boss would never let her marry him. Why,

he'd as soon open the gates and put one of his prize Guernseys out – first come first served,' said Chuck.

'But what if he's Windy's grandson?' shouted Gilly. 'That gives him a name, don't it?'

'Not if it can't be proved.'

'But Letty's telling it for a fact.'

Sid backed him up, 'Sure she is, and get this. All the outside fellers have been let go. But not Joey.'

'Aw – that's just so he can get the pine grove ready for Old Timers'.'

'It could be the Boss and the Missus is gettin' soft on Joey, seein' as she's so stuck on him,' Sid insisted.

Tim, who hadn't spoken so far, now began one of his interminable stories. 'I know a feller who didn't find out who he really was till he was nearly sixty. And then—'

The door opened suddenly and Hank strode in. 'Windy's back,' he announced, 'I just saw him down at the sheep camp.' He went to the counter and began to hunt for something. 'Say – ay – ay,' said Gilly. 'Speak of the devil. We were just talking about him bein' Joey's grandfather.'

Hank jerked around angrily, 'Who says that?'

Gilly, having been hired by Hank, back-tracked. 'Why – it was you, Jim, wasn't it?'

Jim, busy at the stove, replied, 'No, I didn't say it. But it's what I believe all the same. What are you looking for, Hank?'

'A knife with a sharp point. I've got a splinter in my thumb. Jim, you don't really believe that hog-wash do you?'

Jim found the knife and handed it to Hank. 'Sure I do. There's something that ties those two together. Don't know what it is.'

'A lot of bull,' growled Hank and began to dig savagely at his thumb.

61

'But it *could* be true,' yelled Gilly.

'So could I be a pansy,' commented Hank, 'but I'm not.'

'Gad!' exclaimed Gilly. 'Think of the two of them here together at the same time. That ain't never happened before.'

The conversation took on a livelier note.

Hank tossed the knife on the counter and wrapped his handkerchief around his thumb which was bleeding freely. Then he flung himself into a chair and tilted it back against the wall.

He sat listening, saying nothing, his face gloomy and frowning, his chin on his chest.

Just as effective as the African method of spreading news by the beating of great drums, is the method of casting it on to the country grapevine.

Any news about the Heath Ranch was worth listening to. If it was about Letty, to say nothing of a fight over her, it was a headline.

The whole countryside buzzed with it.

Chapter Eleven

Joey's work in the pine grove went well. He looked forward to the noon hour, sure that Letty would come to share it with him.

Sometimes they rode together. On one such day, they made the steep ascent to one of the upland pastures.

Crowning this hill in the distance were five immense boulders which leaned against each other interlocking in so strange a manner that they seemed a single sculptured form. They had become a landmark called The Big Rocks. They overlooked the whole ranch and miles of prairie beyond.

On a long slope the horses stood shoulder to shoulder, nipping at each other playfully, now and then switching a long tail, while their riders sat relaxed in their saddles, contemplating the wide vista before them.

At last they rode slowly down together.

At other times they just picnicked. Letty would bring a feast in a basket.

As Martha had advised they were getting to know each other.

This provided some surprises, not to say shocks. As when one day Joey said, 'Letty, I bin a-thinkin'. Ain't it time I tole yor Poppa?'

They were seated near one of the cleared areas on ground dappled with spots of sunlight and shadow.

Letty paused in the act of returning napkins and cups to the basket.

'Tell him what?' she asked.

'That you an' me aims to git married.'

Letty laughed and fastened the lid of the basket. 'You don't *tell* him that,' she said, 'you *ask* him.'

'Ask im wot?'

'For his consent.'

'An he kin say yes or no?'

'Of course.'

After a few moments' thought, Joey said, 'Effen he says *NO*, Letty, then you an' me, we jess runs off an' gits married anyways.'

He took the basket from her and set it aside, put his arm out underneath her head so she could lie back against it. She stretched out.

'Letty – darlin' – you couldn't never say no to me now.'

She smiled up at him, 'No I couldn't, Joey.'

A breeze rustled in the trees and some leaves fell on her dress. Joey brushed them off, smoothing down the soft pleats.

'Yor dress is jess about the colour of yor hair. Wot colour do you call it?'

'It's pongee.'

'Pongee,' he murmured. He moved a little closer to her. 'Letty, I got money fer you an' me.'

'Money!' exclaimed Letty. 'How'd you get it?'

'The Granny. She tole me, save yer money, Joey, you'll need it some day. An' I seen how the other hands, every pay day, would go to town an' blow every penny on town gals and likker. So I saved it and they's enough fer a marriage licence and weddin' rings and lots more.'

A strange dreamy look came over Letty's face. He kissed her lingeringly.

64

'I kin hev a job at Haskell's as long as I want one an' he's got awful nice little cabins fer his married help. I awreddy picked out one fer you an' me.'

Letty said nothing. She seemed in a dream, not looking at him but smiling a little when he kissed her or smoothed her rose-petal cheek with the back of his forefinger.

A good deal of worldly wisdom had come Joey's way in his short life, and stayed with him. Also wisdom of a different kind. He knew that love and desire are not the same, that each can exist without the other. He knew that when a boy and girl meet and instantly recognize and take possession of each other and know that henceforth they will spend their lives together and are content, all doubt, all searching ended, this is the miracle of love. Each completes the other. Together they make one whole.

He kissed her eyelids.

He was so happy that the balance of joy and sorrow throughout the universe must have been changed.

It was only when he was away from her, alone and lonely in the night, that desire rode him almost unbearably.

Chapter Twelve

Haying was over at last and the crop safely garnered. There had been no serious accidents and no disastrous weather. Big stacks stood where they might be needed for winter use. The great cow barn was full. Relief was in the very air as the ranch settled down into its more leisurely routine.

In the sunny side porch of the ranch house Martha and Jepson had seated themselves for an after break-fast chat. The coffee urn was there on a low table, cups and saucers and all the fixings. Exactly the right time for that talk, thought Martha.

'Jep, I want to talk to you about Letty and Joey Bud.'

'I was just going to say the same thing to you. She ought not to be seeing so much of him. I was going to say something about it to her but I thought a correction of that sort would come better from you.'

'That was what I wanted to talk to you about.'

'Well, my dear, if you don't want to, it's nothing to worry about. He'll be gone soon.'

'When?'

'As soon as he finishes up there in the pine grove. And it'll be high time too. She sees him nearly every day. She ought not to trifle with a man like that. I don't approve of it.'

'She's not trifling with him, Jepson. She's fallen in love with him.'

'Fallen in love? You don't mean seriously in love?'

'I do.'

'Then she can fall out.'

'Oh, Jep!'

'Young people fall in and out of love quite easily. The usual procedure is, send a girl to Europe, or give her a fling in one of the big cities. She's the belle of the ball at one big party, or an attractive man gives her a lot of attention and pays her compliments, and everything is changed. She comes home a different girl.'

'Not always.'

'Martha, you can't be approving of such an impossible, unthinkable marriage! Why, the fellow doesn't even know his father's name. In all likelihood he's a foundling.'

'Letty doesn't think so. She thinks he is Windy's grandson – the one he's been hunting all these years.'

Jepson gave a short laugh. 'I've heard all that nonsense. Just a wild guess.'

'She's convinced of it, Jep.'

'Then she's convinced herself. There's no way to prove such a thing. There couldn't be. Why, Martha, I'd never forgive myself if I let my daughter take such a chance.'

'Jep, there's no way to *disprove* it either.'

'Martha, you're talking as if *you* believe he's Windy's grandson too. But you don't really, do you?'

Martha hesitated. 'Well, it does seem to me unlikely that there would be two boys the same age, lost in the same general area of Wyoming.'

'Not at all. There are probably dozens. Think of all the foundlings that are farmed out for adoption. Wards of the state.'

As if evoked by the talk about him the old Professor rounded the corner of the house and stood before them.

He was, by now, an old friend to everyone on the Heath ranch and they welcomed him warmly and urged him to sit down and have coffee with them.

But he made excuses. 'You're very kind but I won't intrude on you. I'll just stay a minute.'

'Any luck in your search, Windy?' asked Martha, for that was the first thing anyone asked Windy.

'It is about that I have come. Yes, I have news at last.'

'How splendid!' cried Martha, and Jepson said, 'By George! You've struck a trail?'

'Well a possibility. But of course I follow every clue. It was all so long ago, you may not remember but the last that is known of my grandson was that a Mexican sheepherder had him in charge. So I've been hunting Mexican sheepherders all over Wyoming. There are a good many. I heard the other day that there's one not far from your ranch and I thought you might know about him?'

He finished on a questioning note and Jepson shook his head but said heartily, 'If there is such a man in the neighbourhood we'll find out about it. I promise you that.'

The talk was interrupted by Hank who came to tell Jepson that the veterinarian was in the barn for his regular monthly call.

Jepson excused himself immediately to Windy and accompanied Hank, listening to Hank's report of what Doc had to do. Old Nellie was lame. One of the Guernsey cows had split a horn to the root – that would have to be sawed off – and Doc advised de-horning the spring calves.

Windy and Martha, left alone, continued their talk. Windy felt more relaxed now, sat down, and accepted a cup of coffee. It seemed providential to Martha that Windy had shown up on the ranch just when Joey was there. Something might happen to link the two, and Letty's wild guess would come true.

Martha said, 'How wonderful it would be if after all these years, you found your grandson.'

'The strange thing is,' said Windy, 'that though I never saw that little boy, I see him so clearly in my mind's eye that I could describe him to you—'

'Oh, do,' said Martha.

And immediately Windy's manner became animated. 'A tow-head, of course, like Joseph and like me too, before I got this white thatch,' and he ran his hand through the mop of white hair, 'and blue eyes. But it's not so much his colouring and features as the trusting way he looks up at me. The way he puts his little hand in mine to go with me, wherever I go.'

Hank, who had been assisting the veterinarian in the barn, now came to the porch with a message for Windy. 'Doc says there's a Mexican sheepherder running sheep on Section Twenty-five. His name is Nicki Morato.'

Hank pointed at a far-away bluff, in a northerly direction. Windy stood up and carefully took the direction from Hank and when the foreman had returned to the barn, took out a neat little notebook and wrote in the name and place.

Then he turned to Martha and thanked her, saying, 'Hope springs eternal. It may be this Nicki Morato.'

While Windy talked Martha's thought spun off in a different direction. Windy and Joey on the same ranch! They would pass each other! Perhaps stop and look at each other! Not recognition, of course, that couldn't be expected – *but something* surely!

Chapter Thirteen

Kimonos from Japan, negligees from France, teagowns from England evolved, eventually, into the trim informal American garment called a housecoat. It buttoned up and fitted tight like a coachman's coat, and, when made in pretty materials, was attractive and convenient, formal enough for living room or the dinner table, comfortable enough for a nap on the sofa or even a last-minute task in the kitchen. Especially, it was becoming to any one with such a slim waist as Martha had.

It was one of these she was wearing on a night when Jepson came home late after working all evening in the barn helping a cow to deliver her calf.

Martha was ready waiting downstairs with the supper of scrambled eggs, hot toast and tea which he liked on such occasions.

Supper finished, Jepson settled into his big arm chair for one last pipe before he went upstairs. Martha perched on his knee facing him, one foot tucked under her, and said, 'Jep, I've got something to tell you.'

He eyed her speculatively puffing at his pipe, turning his head sideways to blow out the smoke.

'You're going to wheedle something out of me. I can feel it coming.'

'Of course,' said Martha. 'Will your knee get pins and needles? I'll get off if you want me to.'

'Sit still. I'm rather enjoying it. But since I never do

anything you ask, or give you what you want, I wonder that you take all this trouble.'

'Oh, Jep!' said Martha contritely and put her arms around his neck.

He held her a moment, as if indulging her, then released her and said, 'Let me guess. It's something to do with Letty and Jo.'

'Oh, don't call him that, Jep.'

'Joey is a baby name. The Boys don't call him that.'

'But it sounds so ordinary.'

'Is my guess right?'

'Yes, it is,' Martha said. 'Seriously, Letty and I have a plan that will, perhaps, prove that Joey is Windy's grandson. Is that worth taking trouble for?'

'By George! I should say so. Actual proof, my dear?'

'I didn't say we had the proof, I said we had a plan to get the proof.'

'Oh, I see,' said Jepson. He took a pull at his pipe. 'Well, where do I come in?'

'It's you who are going to get the proof. That's what I'm wheedling about,' explained Martha.

Jepson looked amused. 'It sounds interesting. I like to do interesting things.'

'You won't like this.'

Jepson removed his pipe and held it away while his heavy-lidded eyes regarded her with their enigmatic look.

'It's getting more interesting.'

Martha hurried on bravely. 'You remember Windy intended to go up to Section Twenty-five immediately to talk to that Mexican?'

'I do recall that. But he hasn't gone, has he?'

'No, we persuaded him to stay until after Old Timers.'

'Who's we?'

'Letty and Jim and I. The Mexican is sure to come

71

down here for the picnic and Windy can talk to him then – save himself the trip up there.'

'Windy doesn't mind a day's travel. That's all he does. Every day of his life.'

'But this way it will keep him here on the ranch while Joey Bud is here too.'

'And what's the point of that?'

'There will be all this time for Windy and Joey to be here together, perhaps meet, get interested in each other – something might happen.'

'Maybe a bell ring? Or a whistle blow?'

'Something. Who can tell what? It's a pretty close relationship – grandfather and grandson.'

'Has anything happened yet?'

'Not a thing.' Martha was indignant. 'Windy looks right through him.'

'How will you change that?'

'That's the plan, Jep. Force Windy to look at Joey and really see him. Face them up to each other.'

Jepson was astonished and exclaimed, 'Why, Martha, do anything like that to the poor old fellow and he'd go off his beam entirely.'

'Oh, no, he wouldn't. When anyone is as absent-minded as that he just has to be jolted out of it.'

Jepson gave this serious thought, then he said, 'But you could do all this without me. Why not do it yourself?'

'Oh, no, Jep. You're the whole thing.' Martha got off his knee and fetched a tray from a side table. 'Someone has to arrange a suitable occasion and take charge. Ask all the questions. Make him listen and look and think.' While she spoke she was putting the dishes on the tray.

Jepson did not answer immediately. Glancing at him, Martha saw that he was giving consideration to what she had said although with some amusement.

She lifted the tray and carried it to the kitchen. When she returned, she paused a moment in the doorway looking at him searchingly. 'Well, Jep?' she asked brightly.

He was knocking the ashes out of his pipe. 'It might work,' he said, and the bantering note had left his voice. 'It's worth a try, anyway.' He stood up and stretched. 'What a day.'

'Was it a heifer or bull calf?'

'Heifer. That's three heifers in a row for that cow. She's a gold mine.'

They went about the room turning off the kerosene lamps.

Chapter Fourteen

Even more important than Jepson's co-operation would be Windy's, and Martha gave a good deal of thought to the manner of approaching him. She decided that the best thing to do would be to tell her plan frankly. As she began he listened very politely.

'One of our hired hands is a very fine-looking young man. I wonder if you've noticed him?'

'I don't recall,' answered Windy. 'There are a good many young men around.'

Martha continued, 'What might interest you is that he, also, is a lost boy and just about the age your grandson would be. In short, we have been thinking he might be your little lost boy.'

'Not very likely,' said Windy with a slight smile.

'No, of course it is unlikely. But not impossible. I've been wondering how we could find out. He doesn't look anything like you. But he might look like your son Joseph.'

'If he looked like Joseph I should have noticed him.'

'But you may not really have looked at him. Sometimes it is like that, you know. You're looking right at something but you don't see it because you aren't expecting it.'

Windy smiled and waved his hand. 'You are correct, Mrs Heath. Have you something in mind?' So Martha told him her plan. Windy agreed as if it was of no importance.

Next she told Jim Billings.

Jim passed the news on to the Boys for they were all to be spectators. They would see Windy at last forced to look at Joey – really look at him as if he wanted to see him. Look at him the way a man would look at a horse he was going to buy. They were to watch and listen and observe and take part in the final judgement. This was going to be a real show and an air of excited anticipation ran amongst them.

Only one person objected – Joey Bud. But he objected with a violence that threatened to block all Martha's efforts.

Letty added her persuasions to her mother's but Joey went off somewhere and could not be found. It was Jim who finally routed him out and argued with him.

'It's a break for you, kid. A real break!'

'Aw, Jim, it shames me. Like I was a-standin' there a-beggin' him to say I'm kin to him!'

But he gave in at last. He could not help himself.

The plans went forward.

Time and place were important. It would be on the clearing in front of the ranch house after the evening meal. It would still be daylight.

When the time came Windy and Joey took their positions about six feet apart, facing each other. Jepson not far from Windy and Jim Billings close behind Joey.

All the Boys had good vantage points; Joey could feel their eyes boring into him.

Jim said, 'Get close, Joey, look him in the eye. You're as good as he is any day.'

Muttering something unintelligible, Joey moved a few inches closer and stopped.

Windy was unruffled, dignified and superior.

Jepson Heath's voice rang out, 'Now that you are

75

really looking at him, Windy, do you see any resemblance to your son, Joseph?'

'None at all,' Windy answered calmly.

Jepson went on authoritatively, 'Sometimes people who are very unalike still show a family resemblance. Just a flash now and then. Is there anything like that?'

As if puzzled Windy peered at Joey then shook his head. 'Nothing, I assure you.'

Joey pulled back, turning angrily away, but Jim's hand gripped his arm.

'Steady now, boy, you got to go through with this.'

Joey, gritting his teeth, took his place again.

Jepson had another question, 'What about his eyes? A queer colour. I've never seen such a strong blue. Could that be a family trait?'

Windy assumed his professorial manner, 'Blue eyes predominate in the Anglo-Saxon races. All shades of blue.'

He was ready to deliver a lecture but Jepson cut him off, 'Have you thought of your ancestors? Resemblances sometimes skip generations. Now look at Letty. She's nothing like her mother or me ' (there was some laughter at this) 'but she's the image of *my* mother. Might Joey resemble an old family portrait? One of your parents or grandparents? An aunt?'

Windy's lips pursed in a disdainful smile. 'How ridiculous!' he said.

'That's enough!' shouted Joey. He wrenched away from Jim and stepped close to Windy.

'Wot's it to me, old man, eff'n I be kin to you or not! Kin stand in my own boots, and no thanks to you nor nobuddy!'

Then Jepson started to speak but Joey was first. 'Mr Heath, it ain't fair! Puttin' me up like a criminal which I ain't!'

Joey shouted the words furiously then turned and

76

rushed away. Letty, in tears, followed, crying that it didn't matter, it wouldn't make any difference.

Joey's outburst had a strange effect upon Windy. Near him, on the ground, was a box. He sat down on it quite suddenly.

Those shouts – every note, every tone, that same voice had shouted at him fifty years before, his son Joseph! Then too, shouting in anger.

The genes! They cannot lie.

So this was Joseph's boy. This Joey Bud, this illiterate cow-hand was his grandson, and all he had been saying was untrue.

To correct the untruth he got to his feet, ready to cry out, 'No! No! That's wrong! This is Joseph's boy!'

But before the words were spoken he hesitated, then sat down again.

Those words, spoken aloud, would have torn his own life to shreds. No more happy wandering. No more seeking something never to be found, a sort of grail. The whole dream lost.

He sat, silent for a long time.

Letty had returned and went indoors with Martha.

Jepson had made a bee line for the milking barn.

Occasional bursts of laughter came from the bunkhouse where the Boys had reassembled to hash it all over. Hank was triumphant. 'What a slap in the face for Joey,' he gloated.

'Yea boy!' shouted Chuck.

They prepared to tear the subject to pieces.

'Anyone think those two look alike?' cried Hank.

'Sure,' said Len. 'Both of em got two legs and two arms.'

Over the laughter Gilly made himself heard, 'Say, ya know, I see a kind of likeness between those two.'

He was jeered at and raised his voice higher, 'Sure. They got the same kind of class.'

'Class?' repeated Len. 'So's yer own.' But Jim looked at Gilly thoughtfully.

Jim was not taking part in the general discussion. He had uncovered a big yellow earthenware bowl which stood on the back of the stove. It was full of dough, set to rise for tomorrow's rolls. He now began to knead and punch it down.

Hank continued, 'And what a sell for the Boss! Taking all that trouble, asking all those questions then WHAM! Windy busts it wide open with one word, *ridiculous*!'

Hank's hamming got roars of laughter from everyone except Jim who went on punching his dough.

This annoyed Hank and he promised himself he'd tell Jim where to get off later, when they went up to bed. They shared one of the small bedrooms on the second storey of the bunkhouse.

Chapter Fifteen

Jepson took refuge in his barn. It was empty now. Milking was over. There were no soft munchings and breathings, nor the sound of milk foaming into buckets, but it was drenched with the familiar smell of hay and grain and cows, and it comforted him. He sat in his accustomed place at the high schoolmaster's desk with the big ledger opened before him upon which he was accustomed to record the amount of milk each of his prize Guernseys gave. He thought about all that had happened and was satisfied with the part he had played. He had done it for Martha and done it wholeheartedly.

He dwelt for a few moments on the irony of the situation: a man raises a lovely daughter, and lavishes love and care on her amounting almost to adoration. Only to have her stolen from him, when she is grown, by almost anyone.

He ran over the list of Letty's suitors: of course every hired hand he had ever employed, most of them sons of local ranchers; some wayfarers from distant parts of the country, come to try their hands at being cowboys. Then there was that tall, very good-looking nephew of Haskell who had been to Princeton and was now at medical school. And, of course, Hank. Considered as men they were as fine a lot as you would find anywhere. But considered as possible husbands for his daughter he disliked them all.

The one he disliked the least was the one last added to the list, Joey Bud.

This surprised and puzzled him for it was not in his nature to be sorry for people. Fate dealt the cards. A man had to take up the hand he received and make the best of it.

Here was a young man who had everything. Health, strength, looks, brains, skills. He never made mistakes. All this was invalidated because of the lack of a sound pedigree. He was just a foundling and his children and grand-children could be anything.

Expendable! Cross him off the list.

Of course this involved Letty, but he didn't worry about that. A wayward child can be managed. It was Martha who troubled him for she seemed to have gone over to Letty's side one hundred per cent.

After a while he went in search of his wife and found her in the kitchen garden. She was seated on a bench with Letty close beside her.

Letty was tied in a knot. Her arms were clasped around her knees which were drawn up to her chin. Her feet were tucked under her. Her hair was dishevelled and her eyes red and swollen. Her face was turned away from Martha, who was pleading with her.

Martha looked up and gave a little start as she saw her husband, 'Oh, Jep! You startled me.'

'I'm sending Joey Bud away. He'll leave tomorrow.' Jepson said quietly.

Letty looked up at her father, her face expressionless, but Martha exclaimed in surprise, 'But his time isn't up till the day after Old Timers.'

'I'll pay him his full time, two weeks more.'

'But have you forgotten?'

'Forgotten what?'

'Morato! The sheepherder Windy's been looking for!'

'What about him?'

'He'll come to the picnic of course, and Windy and he will talk. That may mean everything to Joey. Letty too. Well, all of us.'

'But Martha! Windy's blown it! You heard him. That changes everything!'

'It doesn't change Morato.'

'Martha, are you still clinging to that? It's an empty hope.'

'Maybe a wild hope, Jep, but not empty. That is, we aren't sure yet.'

'A pretty slim chance.'

'Yes. But it's the only one left now.'

Letty's lips trembled. She looked down, picking at the braid on her mother's skirt.

'All right, he can stay,' said Jepson frowning. 'That'll give him time to finish the work in the pine grove. But there's something I'd like to say about that. Letty is up there with him every day in the noon hour. They ride. Or they lunch together. In the evenings they take long walks. That's the way an engaged couple behaves.'

Letty's face was very white. She said softly, 'Well – we *are* engaged.'

'No, you're not engaged or going to be. You can't be, till I give my consent and I don't give it. Moreover, I don't want it to look as if you're engaged. I don't want you talked about. So cut it out!'

Letty's face did not change but tears ran down her cheeks. 'What do you mean, Poppa?'

'You keep away from the pine grove when he's working there. And no more walks in the evening. Don't go riding with him. Understand?'

Letty didn't answer. She was fighting for control.

'Understand?' repeated Jepson.

Martha intervened. 'Oh, Jep! Of course she

understands. She'll obey you – she always does. Letty?'

'Understand?' he repeated for the third time and this time it was like the flick of a whip.

Letty burst into tears and covered her face with her hands. Through her sobs she said, 'Yes.'

Jepson looked at his wife, 'I'm counting on you, Martha.' He walked away.

Chapter Sixteen

The genes and their strange behaviour had always interested Windy. When he had been a Professor at Harvard one of his lectures on the subject had been famous.

'Consider, young gentlemen, the genes! A fine subject for an essay. How they find their way down the generations, always retaining their identity, their exact individuality with unerring details of physiognomy and musculature. Is this immortality? The genes never grow old. Sometimes they disappear, like a river going underground; appear again in a distant branch of the family when many years have passed. Then it is called a "family resemblance". It comes and goes. One moment it is there – just a sudden flash – then it is gone. Most mysterious but absolutely incontrovertible. Evidence of a blood link that would convince any judge and jury.'

Windy was thinking of this lecture as he climbed the steep narrow trail that twisted up to the Big Rocks.

As yet he had not been able to face up to what he had done. His thoughts were so confused the pain was almost physical. Up there at Big Rocks he could pour out his questions, particularly that one which lay in his breast like a foreign object, hurting.

It would be another trial, this time with no one to watch and listen. When harsh cruel truth is made to come out of hiding and show itself, a man should be alone.

Arrived at the summit, it was Windy's first question and he cried it aloud, 'Had I recognized him before he began to shout at me in Joseph's voice? Did I simply lie?'

After a few moments of silence he gave the answer himself, calm and judicial. 'No. But I let the false verdict stand.'

Where the great stone pillars entered the earth there was a little patch of level ground. Windy began to pace back and forth, flinging out sentences – whole speeches that fell into the silences of the windswept slopes below.

'I cast the spell, then fell under it myself. I pretended. I dreamed the dream. Created the little boy so that now I feel I cannot live without him.

'Now they are talking about a marriage between my grandson and that nice girl.

'So I am robbed of my little boy. What do I do now?' he demanded in a loud voice. 'What am I here for?' and looked around then again answered his own question.

'Why, I am waiting here so that a sheepherder called Nicki Morato can come and tell me about the child.'

He thought this over with a sardonic smile. 'But it is *I* who can tell *him*. The child is here. He is a hired hand. A cow puncher. He is taller than I. And since he has no name he uses an alias, Joey Bud. Nicki Morato and Joey Bud between them are robbing me of my little boy. What will my life be like now? I shall be alone and very lonely.'

Silent once again, his face twisted into an expression of alarm then almost terror. But it was the look of a man struggling with himself and he muttered, 'No, no, no. I did it to myself. There never was a little hand in mine.'

He sat down on a low boulder and bent his head on

his hand. He felt dizzy and it seemed to him he was light-headed, going to faint. And then he was going over backward and falling, faster and faster, plummeting downward between everything that was, into deeper and deeper nothingness. The falling did not stop. It went on until he was off the earth and falling through space. It would never end. All the time he was sitting quietly on the rock, leaning over, his head bent on his hand. Then all consciousness left him and he had the blessed boon of complete oblivion.

While he slept the night passed and a new day dawned.

He stirred, stood up slowly and stretched and saw before him the glorious country of his wanderings. Sunrise poured over the sky painting it with beautiful colours.

Here were the rolling plains that had given him back his health, his youth. He took deep breaths, drawing in the ecstasy.

At last he turned to the trail which had led him to the Big Rocks and began to descend. He reached a point where it forked, one fork leading back to the clearing, the other out on to the plains. He took the latter, walking swiftly with a long free stride as if escaping. He felt stronger as he walked. In an hour he had left the Heath Ranch behind him.

Chapter Seventeen

In the early evening of that same night which Windy had spent at Big Rocks, he was the subject of a long conversation held about him in the second storey bedroom in the bunkhouse which Hank and Jim Billings shared. It was small and sparsely furnished but very comfortable.

Their two white-painted iron beds were flat against opposite walls leaving six feet of bare floor between. On this was spread an oval braided rug which would have been a prize for any antique dealer. The fabric was softest wool. The exquisite colour a blend of ashes, smoke and sand.

These rugs are made by the women of the ranches. Old, worn-out, long underdrawers are cut into inch-wide, bias ribbons which are braided, then sewn together into any shape that was desired. They lay flat on the floor without humping. To get the bias, the cutting had to begin at the bottom of each long leg, then spiral upwards. It was one of these collector's items which filled the space between the two beds.

There was a small round table by the head of Jim's bed and on it a kerosene lamp. Two rather frail-looking wooden chairs with rope seats were seldom used because it was much easier to sit on the edges of their beds facing each other when they wanted to talk as they did tonight.

That is to say, Hank was still savouring the results of the afternoon's spectacle. He went over his recollections of it with melodramatic variations, ending with, 'I almost bust a gut, didn't you, Jim?'

'Well, I don't know,' was Jim's irritating answer.

He was occupied in mending a three-cornered tear of serious proportions in the seat of his trousers.

'But kind of a jolt for you.'

'How so?' Jim held the edges of the tear together and carefully drew the big needle through.

'Your theory shot to bits. About Windy and Joey.'

'Oh, that,' said Jim. 'No, that hasn't changed.'

'What's eating you, Jim!' exclaimed Hank. 'You heard Windy! And I'll hand it to the old man. He told the truth! It was a show-down.'

'He told what he *thought* was the truth,' admitted Jim and held his work closer to the light.

Hank glared. 'I don't get you. He was as sure as a man could be.'

'But he looked like a man walking in his sleep. Didn't you notice?'

'You mean he's kind of nuts? Crazy?'

'Not crazy at all. He's brilliant. But he's under a spell.'

'A spell? Spooks?' Hank glanced around the room and gave an exaggerated shudder. 'Jim, you give me the willies.'

'Oh, not that kind of spell,' said Jim, snipping off his thread and laying his work down. 'Just a dream. But that can be just as strong as ropes and chains.'

'A dream,' said Hank almost plaintively. 'I wish you'd talk sense, Jim.'

Hank was not an ignoramus. In fact he had been to college and Jim had not. But everyone listened to Jim.

'Hank, do you remember last year when we heard that awful hollering and groaning in the next room?'

'I sure do. And when we got in there it was nothing but Tim having a nightmare.'

'He was under a spell. Just a dream. But you remember what a hard time we had to wake him up.'

'Shook him till his teeth rattled,' said Hank reminiscently. 'But we did wake him up. I get you, Jim. That's what the Boss did this afternoon to Windy. Woke him up.'

'He tried to but he didn't succeed.'

Hank flared again. 'What's chewing you, Jim? Why, Windy's answers were flat and final. He knew what he was saying all right.'

'Well, I don't know. It didn't change my opinion.'

'You still think Joey is Windy's lost grandson?'

'Looks that way to me. But I think Joey ought to go up to Section Twenty-five and have a talk with the Mexican sheepherder.'

'Cripes! What for?'

'To find out for sure.'

It was nothing less than a premonition that sank its claw into Hank now.

'Joey can't leave the ranch. He's a hired hand on a job. And he hasn't finished the dance pavilion in the pine grove. That has to be ready for Old Timers. And Old Timers is two weeks from today.'

Jim made no answer but started to prepare for the night. In a minute the light was out, the window open, and the bed springs rattled against the slats as the two men stretched out.

Just before he slept that night an unpleasant thought shot through Hank's mind. All very well to forbid Joey to go but how could he keep Morato from coming? Old Timers was a holiday for everyone in the state.

Hank lay awake a long time trying to imagine what might happen to prevent the Mexican from coming to the picnic.

Chapter Eighteen

A few days later Hank announced that he had some private business to attend to.

Early next morning he saddled a horse and took off for Section Twenty-five.

Superstitions have uncanny power. Never break a mirror, walk under a ladder, give a knife to a friend or sit down thirteen at table.

Moreover they are as catching as mumps and measles. Jim Billings had a hunch that Joey was Windy's grandson, and Hank caught it from Jim. And if this Morato turned out to be the sheepherder in whose house Windy's son had died, and they got together at Old Timers picnic and hashed it over, the truth would come out. Joey would win.

One thing at least could be found out. Was Morato the man or wasn't he? Just go up there and ask him. That was the purpose of Hank's ride.

If he was, there would be more to do. He must be persuaded not to come to the Heath Ranch for the picnic. That, Hank knew would be difficult. In fact, he could not figure out how it would be done, but some idea would come to him, he was sure. Perhaps during the ride up there. He jogged along. It was a beautiful morning.

Meadow larks sprang out of the deep fragrant grass over which he was riding and spiralled, singing of the joy of the morning. The sky was azure, the softly blowing west wind was very sweet.

But Hank saw nothing of all this. He was obsessed with one thought, one urgent desire. To be rid of Joey Bud for good and all. As he rode along he grunted out loud, 'He's a pain in the neck.'

He touched his heel to the horse and picked up the pace.

It was getting hotter. He loosened his shirt at the throat and the kerchief which he wore inside it. He crossed the barranca expertly, dropping his horse from one almost non-existent foothold on the sheer face to another, splashing across the shallow run at the bottom and climbing the opposite side like a fly on the wall.

The ground was rising now. He must have already crossed the section line. Now he approached the headland, a steep rise sparsely covered with trees and shrubs.

He left his horse there at the bottom and worked his way up, finding narrow paths, obviously made by animals. He saw sheep grazing, tended by young boys who wore wide-brimmed Mexican hats.

Arrived at the top he saw the house set back on the small plateau and shaded by a few big trees. As he approached it, he passed an outdoor eating place, a small table set around with brightly painted Mexican chairs. The place swarmed with life. Chickens flapped and cackled in a loosely fenced yard which was flung around the far side of the house. A few pigs grubbed and grunted in a patch of verdure. A very old man sat in the sunshine beside the house, smoking a corn cob pipe.

A hanging brass bell was suspended over the front door. When Hank pulled the cord, the door opened – just a crack – and three small children – all with bushy black curls – peered out, then immediately closed the door and a chorus of childish voices loosed a torrent of Spanish.

It was some time before the door was opened again. This time by Morato himself. He was about forty-five, of medium height, lean and wiry with a thin string of a black moustache on his upper lip. After the customary greetings Morato led the way to the garden table and the two men sat down.

Hank knew the Spanish–speaking people were ceremonious so he held back his questions. They spoke of the weather, the hay crop and the price of sheep.

Morato, with a veiled glance over Hank, asked if he was from the Heath Rancho. Hank told him he was the foreman there.

'Where you leave your horse?'

'At the foot of the cliff.'

'Perhaps you got beezeness wiss me?'

'Well, yes – in a way—' answered Hank.

At that Morato turned his face toward the house and yelled, 'Sofia!'

There was an answering shriek, then a lengthy shouted dialogue in Spanish. This soon resulted in the emergence of a pretty woman of thirty or thirty-five who came towards them carrying a small tray with a bottle and glasses. As she came, she was followed by an old sheep dog who sniffed at the stranger then lay down nearby.

She set the things on the table and Morato introduced her: 'My wife.'

Hank stood up instantly and said, inclining his head, 'Señora.'

He was quite a figure of a man. Handsome, commanding, a little overbearing. Sofia dropped him a deep curtsy. Then she returned to the house and the men were alone.

'You running sheep here?' asked Hank, making his voice casual.

'I got a band.'

'Since when?'

'I take over ziss place last year – why you wanna know?' Morato's voice was a little sharp.

'Where were you before?' asked Hank.

Morato answered stiffly, 'I run sheep many places – Windemere, Elder, Grasso.'

'Windemere!' Hank cut the exclamation short. This must be the man.

With an edge to his voice Morato asked, 'Meester Burro, why you ask me theess ssings? I done some ssing you don' lak?'

'No, no,' said Hank quickly. 'I'm just trying to get some information. You might be able to help me out. Did you ever, long ago, take into your house a man sick with a fever? A feller looked like he was a swell from the East? Had a little boy with him?'

Morato's expression of surprise, growing into amazement, was comical.

'How you know 'bout zat?' he demanded.

Hank's pulse quickened. There could be no further doubt. This was the man. 'The man died, didn't he?' he said.

'Zass right. Zee man died.'

'What happened to the boy?'

A look of regret spread over the Mexican's face and brought a ray of hope to Hank. If tick fever had put an end to both of them then he would never have to worry about Windy's grandson or Joey Bud again.

But that was not what Morato was saying. 'I all ways feel bad 'bout zat leetle keed. I keep 'um a while. But zat veree bad boy. Make me mad. He chase my chickens and ducks. Turn zee hose on zee ole Granpa. Bust zee windows. Worst of all he spoil my sheep dog.'

'How could he do that?' Hank asked.

Morato pointed to the old sheep dog and explained, 'Rigo was a pup zen. I was trainin' heem for a sheep dog. He was doin' fine, taking hold wiss zee sheep lak he know how. Zen comes ziss keed – all my work undone!'

'How was that?' asked Hank.

'Boy fall in love wiss zee pup. Pup fall in love wiss zee boy. Night times, zey sleep on floor togezzer, arms around ees ozzer. Mornings I take zee pup out wiss zee sheep, leave boy home wiss zee chickens. Behind my back, zee dog sneak home to zee boy.' Morato's face became angry as he remembered this. 'I puniss zat dog. I whup heem. I keek heem. Makes no difference. So I give that boy away.'

'Who did you give him to?'

'A man in a Ford. A peddler goes ridin' around to ranchers, selling t'ings. Razors to gentlemens, brazzieres to ladies. He want some bodee to ride wiss heem. He take zat leetle keed an I nevaire see him again. You know anyssing 'bout zat leetle boy, Senor?'

Hank said, 'I know all about him. He's not little any more. He's grown up now.'

'No-no – a leetle keed. 'Bout so high.'

'Yeah – so high – about fifteen years ago.'

'Fifteen years! Madre de Dios!'

'Well, look at your dog. He's no pup now. Can you still use him with your sheep?'

Morato looked at the old dog sadly and shook his head. 'He's pretty old for herdin'. I need a new dog. If I could find a pup this one could train him for me before he die. You know any litters?'

That was when the plan came into Hank's mind, made to order. He spoke slowly, feeling his way, 'We've got a fine litter of sheep dog puppies on the ranch right now. Strathmore border collies.'

The breed was a famous one and Nicki's indrawn breath was almost a gasp. But before he bargained, he remembered to calculate.

After a moment he said, 'I got no money, but I got fine spring lambs. Seex mons old, ready to sell. I giff one lamb for one pup.'

Hank just shook his head.

'Two lambs.'

'Jepson Heath's pups are never for sale.'

'How I get one zen?'

Hank's answer was smooth and casual. 'You do me a favour, and I do you a favour.'

'O-ho! A fay-vor! What I gotta do to get ziss pup?'

'Just one thing. Tell a lie.'

The Mexican was startled. He wanted no trouble with the law though it was hard to know what was and what was not lawful.

'Oh, Señor, I do not like lies. I nevaire tell lies.' Then he realized that, in a way, he was insulting the foreman and added hastily, 'Nevaire except iss necessaree.'

'They are very fine pups,' said Hank laconically.

Nicki peered at him, puzzled. He thought of that puppy. How carefully he and Rigo would train it. He wanted it. He needed it. And it was almost within his grasp.

He began to ask about the lie, not because he intended to tell it, but just to find out about it.

'Ow many words – ziss lie? A lie in many words ees veree hard to remember.'

'Just three words.'

'Tree words? Muss be veree beg lie!'

'That boy we were talking about – you must say that boy died.'

'Zee boy died?'

94

'That's it.'

The longer Morato thought about it the more puzzling it got. Frowning, he scrutinized his visitor. Tall, imposing, the foreman of a rich rancher – was he a crook?

'Meester Burro! Zis lie *stinks*! Killing pipples iss bad beezness.'

With an exasperated grunt, Hank said, 'There's no killing about it. I told you. He's alive. He's grown up.'

'Lies ees all ways to cover up some bad sing.'

'What harm could it do now? It all happened long ago.'

'Perhaps nossing. Still smells bad.'

'What a fuss about three words! I didn't think you were such a sissy.'

'Maybe a sissy. Maybe juss too smart for feeshy beezness,' answered Nicki calmly.

'What's so fishy about it?'

'Maybe you keel heem yourself?'

Hank exploded, 'Morato, you're all mixed up! You're thinking it's a different boy!'

'You keel sombodee else?'

Hank threw up both hands. 'Let's begin all over. I asked you, "What happened to the boy?" and you said you gave him to a man in a Ford. And they rode away together."'

'So pliss tell me, Meester Burro, why I gotta say zee boy died?'

'That's the whole point. That's the lie. To get the dog.'

Hank settled back with the air of one who has explained a great mystery.

Morato averted his eyes and hung his head a little, as mystified as ever. All he could be sure of was that Meester Burro was not to be trusted; and as for lies – some meant nothing. Others, you could hang for.

'Meester Burro, eef no killing, eef nossing bad, no harm to nobodee, w'y you *want* I tell ziss lie?'

Hank was embarrassed. 'Oh, it's just a sort of trick to help patch up a love affair.'

Nicki stared at Hank in astonishment, a smile dawning on his face. 'Love? Love affair?'

Hank explained further, 'A love affair that's gone wrong.'

This changed everything for the Mexican. He smiled at the thought of this arrogant but handsome man having trouble in a love affair. Smiled at the thought of that puppy which might be his.

'But Meester Burro, in love affairs iss always lying.'

'That's a fact.'

'Don't smell bad at all.'

'Why should it?'

'Meester Burro, *eef* I tell ziss lie, who I gonna tell it to?'

Hank hesitated. Before leaving the ranch that morning, he had known that Windy had disappeared. No one could be sure of his return. If he did not show up who would ask Morato the questions? The Boss, of course. Martha and Letty would make him. So he said, firmly, 'Jepson Heath.'

'Oh-ho! Jepson Hees! He's beeg man 'round 'ere. W'en I gonna see heem?'

'You going to Old Timers picnic?'

'Sure I go. Everee bodee goes.'

'That's when you'll see him. He'll ask you those same questions I asked you and when he says "What happened to the boy?" that's when you'll say—'

Nicki interrupted as if trying it out before committing himself to tell it, 'Zee – boy – died—'

96

'That's it.'

'Veree easy lie to remember.'

'Nothing to it.'

'An *eef* I tell eet wen do I get zee pup?'

'That same day at the picnic. I'll meet you on the path outside the picnic grounds at four o'clock. And I'll have the puppy with me.' Hank stood up. 'Well?' he said.

'Eef I *don't* tell eet—'

'You don't get the dog.'

Nicki rose slowly and they faced each other. There was a long silence.

'Anything else you want to know?' Hank asked restraining his impatience.

Nicki answered with dignity. 'Now I gonna make up my mind.'

Hank chewed at his lips. He said, 'Don't be in a hurry.' And there was another period of deliberation.

At last some unknown quantity tipped the scales and the decision was made.

'I gonna do it.'

Hank seized his hand. 'It's a deal.'

Hank picked his way down the cliff to the bottom where he had left his horse, mounted and rode home.

Nicki hastened to find his wife and tell her proudly of the good business deal he had made, how he would get a fine young sheep dog and practically free. But Sofia said, 'Not free, Nicki. You pay for heem wiss a lie. Money iss better.'

'I *got* no money!' shouted Nicki.

That was the day that Martha and Letty drove to Denver to buy their costumes for Old Timers. The shops there were as good as any in the country.

Martha's was of jade-green chiffon, most becoming to her dark loveliness. Letty's was of cream brocade,

97

cut so as to simulate panniers, and very pretty on a dance floor.

Jepson's suit had already been made. It was in semi-military style with a waist-length battle jacket and standing collar. The material was sand-coloured gabardine.

Chapter Nineteen

To refer to it as a picnic hardly did it justice. The term would not suggest the polished limousines of the Governor of the State or the State Senators to say nothing of the private railway car of the President of the Union Pacific Railroad. It was a grand affair, a big party given once every year by the railroad somewhere along its tracks. Property owners whose land was chosen for the site considered themselves honoured.

In the early days when the cattle men had taken the land from the buffalo herds, it had been the Union Pacific which had linked up with an eastern system and so achieved trans-continental train travel for the first time.

That linking up was a ceremony like a wedding. Crowds were watching when the last spike was driven which fastened the last length of steel to the last wooden tie. The spike was of pure gold, as all wedding rings should be.

From such historic events the railroad men, both officials and working crews, got their name, Old Timers.

In time younger men replaced the old ones and still were called Old Timers. It became a sort of hereditary elite and finally carried over to the event itself.

'Are you going to Old Timers?' people would ask and everyone would know they meant the picnic.

The pine grove on the Heath ranch where it was to be given this year contained a siding and actually

99

straddled the tracks. Also, among the trees, were ample cleared spaces for games and races. It was in every way an ideal location.

As the day approached, newspapers in Cheyenne and Windemere carried notices. On the roads, signposts were erected, pointing the way.

On the Heath Ranch preparations had been under way for weeks. Every foreseeable demand had been met. As for those unforeseeable accidents and emergencies which were bound to occur when such a large crowd was gathered in one place, Jepson Heath would have to deal with these. He accepted the responsibility without much concern.

What bothered him more was a private matter. Here it was, the day before the picnic, and Windy had not yet returned.

Not that he expected anything to come of the meeting between Windy and the sheepherder but Martha and Letty did. So it nagged at him. He could not be rid of it.

Of course Windy came and went as he pleased and would probably show up before it was too late, but this was cutting it close.

Martha thought so too. Before she went to bed that night she went in to Letty's room and found her daughter sitting by the window, staring out, a very sombre look on her face. Her hair was not braided; a thin wrapper covered her nightgown.

Martha sat down on the edge of the bed. 'You should get to bed, dear. There's no use in sitting here brooding.'

'Momma, what if Windy's forgotten all about it?' answered Letty.

'Oh, I think Windy will show up, dear. After all, he's been hunting for this sheepherder for a long time.'

'But if he doesn't, who will talk with Morato?'

'Your Poppa.'

'Poppa won't want to do that.'

'Your Poppa will do it,' promised Martha staunchly.

'And Momma, of course there's always the possibility that Morato's not the right one.'

Letty spoke of this dire possibility so calmly that Martha was alarmed. 'Why then, dearie, you'll just have to wait. You and Joey.'

There was a long silence. Then Letty pulled her chair around to face her mother.

'I hate to say this, Momma, but when Joey leaves day after tomorrow, I'm going with him.'

Martha opened her mouth to reply then shut it. She looked at her daughter helplessly. There was something about Letty tonight that was frightening. At last words came.

'You mean you would be married somewhere else? Not at home?'

'Yes. In Cheyenne. We've got it all planned.'

'Oh, Letty! You can't mean that! You wouldn't do such a thing!'

A torrent of words poured from Letty.

'It's as if Joey and I had been looking for each other all our lives. And that morning when we found each other – I told you all about it – how we fell in love and were so happy for a while—'

'Cheyenne,' gasped Martha, 'Cheyenne! Oh, Letty! Not Cheyenne.'

'Then Poppa ordered us to keep apart. It was that day in the kitchen garden. You remember, Momma. You were there.'

'Of course, I remember! And you promised your father you would obey him!'

'It isn't fair to remember just that! He made me, forced me. Of course I didn't obey him. I disobeyed him.'

Martha's face went white. She said in a shocked whisper, 'You disobeyed your father!'

'Of course. Joey and I got together every day in one of my hideaways.'

'Oh, Letty!'

'But we had to, Momma, can't you understand? We're going to get married!'

'But not immediately,' pleaded Martha. 'Letty, a girl's marriage is so important. To have it in her own home, her parents happy about it, her friends around her, the presents and all the fixings. Why, you'll remember it all your life. You'll keep your wedding dress and veil laid away in a box with blue tissue paper, and some day you'll show it to your children.'

Letty listened, unmoved, her face strained and sad. 'But it won't be like that. Because Joey has to leave day after tomorrow.'

'But Letty, you don't have to go with him. Not now. He can come back for you when things have been arranged, when your Poppa ...'

'Poppa won't change. Nothing will change. I wouldn't dare to let Joey and me be separated.'

'Why? A separation would give us all time to think things over. That never hurts.'

'No, Momma. When people who ought to be together get separated things happen to keep them apart and it's as if they can never find each other again.'

There was a long silence. Both of them felt unseen forces pushing them around and there was nothing they could do about it.

At last Letty said sadly, 'When the time comes for me to go, I'll not come to say good-bye to you, I'll just be gone.'

The words had a dreadful finality. The chill of them surrounded Martha like a cold breath and she shivered. Protests and pleadings clamoured in her mind but died unspoken, as if it was too late. The deed was already accomplished.

At last she leaned forward, kissed her daughter and left the room. She closed the door behind her and stood for a moment leaning against it.

In a crisis she always called to Jepson for help. But Letty had disobeyed him once and might do so again. This was a new Letty. In fact, this was a woman. And unless Jepson changed his way of dealing with her he would only harden her determination.

Obviously, no one could influence her now except Joey. He was, in fact, in total command of the situation.

Anger boiled up in her.

Frustrated, blocked in every direction, she stood trembling, violent emotion overcoming her usually logical thinking. There was simply nothing she could do.

After a long while she walked slowly down the corridor.

Chapter Twenty

The day of the picnic dawned bright and warm. The sky was clear except for one large dark cloud which hung directly over the ranch. As if to show what it could do, it released a light shower early in the morning. This was a blessing, and settled the dust.

Letty did not go down to breakfast, but Jepson and Martha, Hank and Jim got up early and drove to the pine grove to make final inspections.

They intended to choose a location which should be a headquarters for the Heath family and staff, a sort of outdoor lounge far enough from dance pavilion and band stand to give respite from the noise, but near enough to the cleared areas for a view of the games. Here, someone would be on duty all day, ready with iodine and bandages or thread and needles.

Joey Bud was also in the pine grove that early morning although at some distance from the others, clearing away the last vestiges of the work he had done there.

He was already in costume for the dance.

The sun had faded Joey's bluejean suit to a pale, misty blue. It had also shrunk it. He looked as if he had been poured into it. He wore a sprig of blue larkspur in his jacket. It grew wild on the Wyoming plains, and the colour – an intense deep blue – was the exact colour of his eyes, startling in the expanse of tawny skin and hair.

He looked fine enough for any fancy dress party and as for dancing, he had the know-how. Besides that, a good ear for music. Time and rhythm were in his blood.

In rural areas parties were very frequent, and they were for all, young and old, so the training began when they were tots. Few people needed dancing school.

All the Boys on the Heath Ranch were good dancers. It would be wonderful fun to take girls on to the dance floor when the band began to play. Not so much fun when it was old-ish women, important and probably fat, or stiff and angular and hard to lead. But that would be their duty.

Joey wondered what would be expected of him. Dance? Or not. He did not care. Today did not matter for tomorrow was close.

He was strung up tight, waiting for it.

Then he saw that Mrs Heath had left the others and was walking toward him. Martha had not been able to get over her anger of the night before, and it still seethed in her.

Joey straightened up at her approach, ready to greet her pleasantly. Then, appalled by the look on her face, he stiffened and stood rigid, stunned by her words.

'You'd think a man could see it for himself. Take a girl away from her home and all her people when he has none of his own to make up for it! A licence at City Hall instead of a wedding! Not even a real last name of his own for the children! Why! If you take her away with you against our will, without our consent, she'll have an ache in her heart as long as she lives!'

The terrible words reached his ears, his nerves and every drop of blood in his body.

Martha turned away from him.

She did not rejoin the others but went to the car in which they had driven out from the ranch to the pine grove.

She got in, leaned back and closed her eyes. The

hands lying in her lap were both clenched and her heart was pounding.

A little later Jepson came back to the car. 'We found a good place,' he said cheerfully, starting the engine. 'That'll help us get through the day.'

'They'll be coming soon now,' said Martha and her voice sounded almost natural.

Jepson sighed, 'Yes. Time we got into our glad rags.'

Before eleven o'clock cars began driving into the pine grove. Trucks, motor cycles, family cars of ancient vintage or spanking new, little sidecars that zipped down the tracks and were lifted off at the siding. The big cars of the important railroad officials and the political figures would come later.

The nearest military post was Fort Warren, fifty miles away. The officers would come in their fast, low-hung grey cars and they would all be in uniform. It would add style and dash to the gathering.

As the day wore on it looked more and more like a fancy dress ball for if the people were of all sorts their costumes were more so.

It was the custom for the women to come in clothes which had belonged to their ancestors. So the trunks in the attics had been ransacked and the women appeared in trains, fichus, bustles and basques that had belonged to their grandmothers.

There was also a group of young girls attired in flesh-coloured leotards, their flowing hair making them look like people out of a painting of the Garden of Eden.

There were some eastern 'dudes' who wore breeches that were pouched and baggy above the knee instead of Cheyenne pants. There would be visitors from overseas too.

The big event of the day was the picnic lunch.

Barrels of beer, sides of beef barbecued to sizzling perfection, big pots of chilli, pickles, pies and cakes. An even greater event was when Number Twenty-Nine came through.

Number Twenty-Nine was the fastest train on the line and often carried celebrities from Hollywood to New York.

Today it would be carrying no less a person than America's sweetheart, Mary Pickford. As the time approached, everyone was on the alert, listening.

Suddenly someone yelled, 'There she comes!' There were more shouts and a scurry to clear the tracks for she would go right through the pine grove. Silence now, a breathless waiting, everyone standing and straining their ears.

Then came the sound they were waiting for. Very faint and from far away, the sound of a fast express train approaching at top speed.

'She's over the summit and coming faster than the dickens on the downgrade!'

Faster and faster, closer and closer, until suddenly she was upon them with a roar like an earthquake, the wheels pounding like drums, the wind of her passing stirring up a storm of dust, leaves and gravel.

The last car whipped out of sight, the roar diminished, she was gone. And when the whistle came it was wafted back from a distance, a long, hollow receding wail that carried a strange note of fatefulness, exciting and yet sad.

The echoes died away slowly.

On this occasion there was another echo. A long trembling wolf howl which seemed to come from a distant peak of the Rocky Mountains. Everyone roared with laughter.

Someone imitated the long drawn wolf howl. Someone else howled on a higher note. It caught on, and suddenly there was a whole wolf pack howling including even the frantic yappings of coyotes.

It broke up in more laughter and then settled back into the strange, sustained, cackling buzz which characterized these merrymakings.

Jepson Heath stood listening to it and judged by its intensity that the party was a huge success. Everything had gone well so far. Only one drunken brawl and that one he had been able to quell easily.

Swede had come up to him once, 'Hear that bawling, Boss? A feller came in with a truckload of calves, taking them to market. Wants to know if he can stay at the picnic a couple of hours.'

'Nothing doing,' snapped Jepson. 'Get him out. *Pronto*.'

'Thought so.' Swede went away.

The heavy cloud overhead had suddenly turned dark and spattered the grove with huge drops. But nothing came of it. The sun shone again and all was as before.

At noon Letty had appeared in the pine grove dressed in her beautiful brocade dress. She went around in a friendly and sociable manner greeting friends and guests, ready with lollipops for a screaming child. But Martha noticed her pallor, the blazing excitement in her eyes, the strange alienation in her face, and knew that her resolve to leave the ranch with Joey the next day had not changed.

Jepson looked at the handsome gowns worn by his wife and daughter and thought to himself with satisfaction, cost me a pretty penny – but worth it.

At two, a large bus arrived from Fort Warren with the band. Soon they began to play and couples drifted towards the dance pavilion. Before long the floor was crowded.

Jepson was deep in conversation with Mr Clutterbuck, the British livestock breeder from whom he had bought much of his foundation stock, and Martha, meanwhile, entertained Mr Clutterbuck's wife and daughter.

Letty was on the dance floor and her partner was Joey Bud. One more disobedience was a trifling matter now.

Letty was on her own now. But something was the matter with Joey and nothing that she said to him could change it.

Exhausted, she lay against him like a wilted flower. When the music stopped, they sat down on one of the benches which were arranged around the dance floor.

Other people, noisy and chattering, crowded around them, squeezed against them, shut them in. They were alone.

'Oh, Joey, why do you keep on saying dunno – dunno – to everything I ask you?'

'Dunno, Letty.'

'And why do you look that awful way?'

He did indeed look awful. Bewildered, strained, all boyishness wiped from his face. He gave her a true answer.

'Cuz, Letty, Eff'n I ain't fitten to be yor husband—'

'Oh, they've always said that!'

'But eff'n it's true then I got no right to take you with me tomorrow.'

'But we've got it all planned! Elope to Cheyenne, then Haskell's!'

'I ain't so sure, Letty, I dunno, I dunno—'

'Momma's been talking to you. She said all those same things to me.'

'Your Momma made me see it like I never seen it before. Oh, darlin'—' He reached for her hands.

'Oh, don't call me those pet words and then say such awful things!'

He could only lean closer to her and say them again.

'Joey, we've talked this all out before.' She was pleading now. 'About your name – Bud. It was our first fight. It was awful. And I said, "What's good enough for you is good enough for me."'

'But, Letty, eff'n I ain't fitten—'

'Oh, don't say it again!' She was near tears.

The music began again. She stood up.

'Let's dance.'

They moved out on to the floor and he took her in his arms. His strong right arm encircled her and held her a few inches from his body. His touch was a caress, she felt the desperation of his yearning.

She whispered, 'Joey, don't we belong together?'

'We sure do. I recognized you fer my own girl the fust moment I seen you.'

'We both did.'

He held her closer. It was just the whisper of an embrace but they both felt the keen sweetness of it to the tips of their fingers and toes.

'Oh, Joey, take me with you.'

'Sweetheart – my little love – I ain't sure—'

'Take me with you.'

They did not dance again.

They left the pavilion and wandered about. They met Gilly who grabbed Joey.

'Say, Joey! What do you think? That Mexican, Morato, he's come! I seen them getting out of their car! His wife – dressed up like a horse and about a dozen kids.'

'Any sign of Windy?' Letty asked.

Gilly shook his head, 'Nope. But there's time yet.'

Letty and Joey wandered on. Found a bench secluded under trees, sat down and waited and wondered and listened to the distant music.

Chapter Twenty-One

For Nicki Morato getting himself and his family to the picnic at all was no easy business. Good luck was needed, but there was bad luck.

A wife's approval is like a warm sun shining. Sofia's disapproval of his good business deal put the sun under a cloud.

Then there was the car, a small two-door sedan. Seating arrangements must be decided in advance so there would be no quarrelling at the start. Sofia would of course sit beside him on the front seat holding Mimi, their youngest.

His two young nephews, Carlos and Tonio, would be in the back seat holding Evita, four years old, and Bettina, five. They would be crowded, for the boys were well grown, but they were strong and could do it.

The old sheep dog, Rigo, could not accompany them. He would be disappointed for he loved to ride in the car with his head hanging out the window. He would be shut up in the chicken yard.

But when Morato went out, early in the morning, to attend to these matters and sweep out the car he found Rigo already in it, sitting up, bright and alert, on the front seat.

Morato was exasperated. But he knew that animals have the gift of foreknowledge. Probably the old dog already knew about the little pup they would be bringing home with them that evening. After all, his own destiny was bound up in it. He would let the dog stay. Sofia would be a little crowded.

But Sofia did not want to sit on the front seat between Nicki and Rigo. This became apparent at the moment of departure and caused considerable delay. Everyone suggested something different, at length, and at the top of their lungs.

'I will sit with Mimi in the back between Carlos and Tonio. We will be packed in tight. That will keep us from bouncing around,' decreed Sofia shrilly.

'Suit yourself,' said Nick.

He walked around the car giving each wheel a kick to test the pressure. It was not going to be a silent ride.

Movement in this car was always accompanied by sounds of clattering and thumping. The sounds had a sort of rhythm and they were all used to it. There were also human sounds. The children never stopped chattering or squealing, laughing or howling. The boys shouted and argued. Sofia only screamed when she had to, to drown the others, or when there was an emergency, which was nearly always.

The car itself was an emergency. Not one real Ford but an amalgam of several, put together with originality and considerable engineering skill.

This car now had to be driven across plains that had no roads or signs. There was a big barranca to cross. To detour around this would add miles to the trip and defeat its whole purpose.

Morato had not forgotten his deadline. To reach the Heath ranch by four o'clock he would have to drive fast. But that was nothing. He always drove with the throttle down as far as it would go, with sand and gravel flying at the sudden, unexpected turns and the occupants of the car swinging and bouncing as he went over big bumps.

Now they were all fitted in. Morato gave three blasts

of the horn, echoed by the full chorus, and the perilous descent began.

They went swiftly, with no more than had been expected of surprises and emergencies, until they reached the barranca.

The runway which led down was narrow and the wheels seemed to slip over the edge. The car tilted. Sofia screamed piercingly.

'Better you should pray, Sofie.'

Down – down – and into the water at last, still upright.

'Now pray we get up zee ozzer side.'

'Hail Mary, full of grace—'

The difficult drive was finally accomplished. The car, still in one piece, was parked in a well-chosen, secluded spot in the pine grove of the Heath Ranch.

The occupants poured out. Rigo trotted around the car spraying each wheel. Morato called him back.

'Get in, Rigo. You gonna stay now.'

The dog obeyed. Nicki gave Sofia her orders. 'Find the picnic tables. I join you later.'

They had not lunched and their stomachs were hungry and growling but Sofia said, 'Why do you not come with us?'

'I have business to do.'

'I do not like this Meester Burro.'

'Woman's like or not-like has nothing to do with it. It is a good business deal.'

'If you say so.'

'I say so.'

Sophia bowed her head obediently.

As soon as the picnic tables emptied of food they were restocked. They were richly laden as the Morato family seated themselves and began to fill their plates. They could hear the band playing at a distance and Sofia began to tap her foot.

She was dressed in a sumptuous yellow satin dress, and Nicki had given her a large, beautiful tortoiseshell comb to hold up her coil of black hair. Over this comb she had draped a black lace veil which cascaded down over the yellow satin.

She had dreams of dancing with the Governor of Wyoming. Now if the band leader would call a number to be Ladies' Choice....

Meanwhile Nicki went about his business. It did not take him long, and when he came back to the car he was carrying a bundle covered with a sack.

He opened the door of the Ford, threw off the sack and thrust the whimpering puppy in.

'Here, Rigo. A little one for you to take care of. See him, Rigo?'

Rigo was instantly up, alert, stiff, reaching out his nose. The puppy gave a long, frightened squeal. Morato pushed them together, his voice reassuring and comforting, then closed the door.

Rigo smelled the puppy all over, nosing and nudging him. They talked to each other, little whimperings from the puppy, low rumbles from Rigo. At last all the proper questions had been asked and answered and they accepted each other. They curled up together on the floor. The puppy relaxed against Rigo's shaggy hide and fell asleep.

Chapter Twenty-Two

For Nicki the most difficult part of the enterprise was still to come. He had the puppy in his physical possession but did not own him until he had told the lie. To do that he had to obtain the co-operation of someone else – no less a person than Jepson Heath himself.

Mr Heath had to ask him questions.

Hank had assured him it would be easy. They would be looking for him. Just walk around carelessly near their family hang-out.

'They'll nab you,' Hank had said.

Like all Latins he took naturally to acting and was not at all averse to drawing attention to himself and his finery. He wore embossed boots, an overblouse of mixed orange and red and a big Mexican hat with rolled-back brim.

But there was much finery around. And suppose nobody nabbed him?

He walked near the Heath gathering place, where Swede darted out. 'Morato! Where you bin? We've been looking everywhere for you.'

'I juss now come.'

Swede took his arm and led him to Jepson Heath who said, 'Ah, Morato, I am glad to see you.'

Nicki swept off his hat, bowed to Mr Heath, then a lower bow to the lady in bright green who stood beside him.

'I have some questions to ask you.'

'You ask, Mr Hees. I weel answer.'

Nicki then noticed out of the corner of his eye that a couple, a beautiful golden-haired girl in white and a tall boy, had moved closer to the group as if to listen.

'Did you ever, a long time ago, take into your house a man who was sick with a fever? Had a little boy with him?'

'Oh, yess, Meester Hees. I remember veree well. Tick fee-vor.'

'The man died, didn't he?'

'Si, Señor, zee man die.'

'What became of the boy?'

'Zee boy die too.'

A number of things happened then, all bad. The lady in green gave a strange sharp cry.

A really terrible scream came from the beautiful girl. She threw herself across the tall young man, holding both his shoulders as if to protect him from all harm.

Mr Heath exclaimed, 'Died! Poor Windy. All those years of searching for nothing!'

And a sort of moan came from everyone.

But worst of all was the transformation of Meester Burro. Nicki stared at him, horrified. That face! Bad. Evil. Mean. Showing his teeth in a snarl while he looked at the young couple and cried triumphantly, 'And there's the proof that Joey Bud is nothing but a catch colt!'

Morato was not slow-witted. He saw it all in a flash. Indeed, anyone could have.

The young couple, so much in love. The foreman, jealous and vengeful, cooking up a scheme to shatter their happiness. A shady, dirty scheme.

And Nicki himself deceived and cheated and drawn into it.

The young couple now disappeared among the trees. Nicki walked over to Hank. 'You play a trick on me?'

116

Hank took no notice of him. Nicki raised his voice and seized the foreman's arm. 'Some feeshy beezness here!'

Angrily, Hank wrenched his arm free and swept the Mexican aside. The violent action caught Nicki off balance and knocked him down.

This caused a commotion for it looked like a fight, and several of the Boys started forward.

But Morato picked himself up quickly, unhurt but slightly dazed. He stood a moment, then turned to look at Hank who was scowling.

Their eyes met and held as if they were calculating how the score stood between them.

Then Morato turned away, pushed through the group and left the meeting place. He disappeared among the trees.

Now he hurried to his car, opened the door and reached for the puppy.

'I'm taking him now, Rigo. It's finished,' he said as he closed the door.

Rigo stood up, stretched and yawned, then turned to the window, lifting his head and sniffing. The air was fresh. He stood on his hind legs and put his front paws on the frame of the window and stuck his head out. The wind blew past his face.

He stood so for quite a long while, then sprang out and loped away.

When Nicki got back to the group, there was at first astonishment and silence. Then a few words rang out which were to be laughed about and mimicked for many a day to come.

'Take back your pup! I take back my lie!'

Morato was standing before Hank, holding a small puppy in the air, offering it to him. A thundering voice which could only belong to Jepson Heath cried out, 'Pup! Lie! What's the meaning of this?'

Hank took the puppy automatically, not knowing what he was doing. Then he started away with it, wanting only to get out of sight as fast as he could. He shouted over his shoulder as he went, 'I was just showing it to Morato. He's been looking for one.'

Nicki said proudly, 'Boy did not die. Did not even get seek.'

'Then what did happen to him?'

Nicki hesitated. 'Ees veree long storee.'

Jepson's voice rose, 'What happened to that child?'

'Si, Señor. Wass long ago when my sheep dog was a yong pup. I was trainin' heem for herdin' an' he was doin' fine. Zen comes zis boy. Everee ssing spoiled. Zey fall in love. Cannot make zem leave ees ozzer. No more trainin' wiss zee sheep for Rigo. Wot a bad boy. I bawl heem out. I whup heem. I keek heem.'

'The boy?'

'No Señor, zee dog. Makes no difference, so I give heem away.'

'The dog?'

'No, Señor, zee boy. A man come drivin' in a Ford. He take zat boy wis heem, juss for company and I nevaire see heem again.'

There was a long moment of silence.

Then Jepson Heath said grimly, 'That puts us right back at the beginning.'

For a while they all talked at once. Then Jim Billings said, 'Say, Morato, where'd you get that puppy? Wasn't it one of ours?'

Morato did not answer immediately. He frowned, thinking it over. They had not blamed him for the lie, or so it seemed. Perhaps they had told a few themselves when it was necessary.

It was the moment to put the blame on Meester Burro, but that he did not intend to do either. It was beneath a man's dignity to admit that the wool had

118

been pulled over his eyes and so he had been drawn into a shady, tricky business.

So he said, 'Rigo veree old now. Too old for herdin'. But before he die he could train up a pup for me. But I got no pup. So I make a beezness deal.'

There were some laughs and comments at that. Jepson Heath said sardonically, 'Apparently, with my foreman.'

Jim put in a word for his room mate, 'Guess Hank figured all's fair in love and war.'

Mr Heath went on, 'And the deal went through. You got the pup. Why did you go back on it?'

Of all the questions this was the hardest to answer and Nicki was silent. He could not explain his concern when that lovely girl had given the terrible scream and thrown herself on her lover's breast.

At last Nicki said hesitantly, 'Zere iss a yong ladee. Veree beautiful. Hair, veree gold. A white dress—' and spread both hands at his sides, shaping the panniers.

Mr Heath interrupted, coldly and sharply, 'My daughter. How does she come into this?'

Nicki saw that the young couple were there again, at the edge of the trees. The young man stayed where he was but the girl came forward and spoke to him.

'Mr Morato, you say you never saw that little boy again. But that's not true. You are looking at him now.' And she pointed to Joey.

Nicki was first astonished then amused. It would be rude to laugh but it was hard to keep his face straight.

'Oh, no, no, Señorita. Zees leetle keed veree oglee.'

Letty persisted, 'But that was fifteen years ago. People change.'

But Nicki, smiling, kept shaking his head. 'Zat oglee leetle keed – nossing like ziss beautiful man.'

His hat was swept off again and this time his deep bow was to Joey.

Meanwhile a big dog was running loose among the crowd. He ignored tit-bits of food offered him, or calls from children who were also running around loose. Sometimes his nose was on the ground as if following a scent, sometimes it was lifted high, smelling the wind.

Often short yelps escaped him. Broken agonized yelps.

Since early morning of that day he had known of the blissful event that was coming – reunion with the playmate he had romped with, played with, and slept with fifteen years ago.

When the moment came and the dog launched himself through the air at Joey, it looked like an attack and there were some frightened yells. Joey staggered as the weight of the dog hit his chest.

Morato sprang forward, crying, 'Down, Rigo! Down!'

But Letty held the Mexican back.

She had seen a strange look on Joey's face, for even as he thrust out both fists to ward the dog off, recognition was dawning.

'Oh! – Oh! – Oh!   Yaller dawg! Yaller dawg!'

Rigo, up on his hind legs, was crying almost pitifully.

With full recognition, Joey's arms went around the dog. The two embraced, hugging each other tight, while Rigo licked Joey's face and neck and ears.

There was pandemonium among the onlookers.

Letty cried, 'Oh, Momma!' and ran to her mother.

Jepson Heath drew in a long breath, then let it out very softly and exclaimed, 'I'll–be–darned!'

Jim Billings said, 'Well, Boss, what about proof now? Is that enough?'

Jepson exploded, 'I should say so! The best proof in the world.' He turned to his wife, 'Martha—' But she was not there.

At a little distance she and Letty were clutching each other, Letty sobbing and Martha holding her hand-kerchief to her eyes.

Jepson went to them and put his big arms around both of them and held them and hugged them as if he had them safe back after a long parting.

The Mexican's exclamations of amazement had been continuous. At last he came to the end.

'Rigo tell us zee truss! Rigo cannot lie because he iss not a man. He iss only a dog.'

Chapter Twenty-Three

There are places in Wyoming where one actually has the sensation that the earth is round.

Perhaps it is the sky which is not like a canopy up there but like a great inverted bowl curving down to meet a horizon which seems lower than the ground you are standing on.

At midnight this inverted bowl is dark velvety blue and filled with blazing stars. Now, at seven, it is light grey with a metal sheen, and there are as yet no stars.

The harvest moon had been promised by the almanac for seven o'clock. It was practically a necessity for a party like Old Timers Picnic, giving light during the long twilight hours ahead. And far more ornamental than Japanese lanterns. But it was already after seven and there was no moon. Just where it ought to appear, there were, instead, darkish clouds. Perhaps it was behind them.

Cars were leaving the picnic grounds and the crowd was thinning out. But the musicians, having eaten and rested, were ready to play again.

Just as they began the clouds parted. There was the harvest moon, a huge yellow globe, sitting on that low horizon as if resting for a moment before taking off for the long journey across the sky.

The picnic crowd yelled and cheered, it would make all the difference.

Another promised guest was late and hardly to be hoped for at this hour.

This was Windy who was making his way to the Heath Ranch, but hardly seeing where he was going because of the pressure of the thoughts that had boiled in him for the last fortnight.

He walked more slowly as he approached the pine grove knowing that the announcement he had to make would bring a storm of reproaches.

To explain seemed almost impossible. Who would understand? No explanations then, but just tell them.

His steps quickened. Suddenly he was there in the midst of them, Jepson Heath, Martha, all the Boys. He said, 'Mr Heath, I have come to make an important announcement.'

There was a guffaw of laughter from several of the Boys, and Jim Billings cried, 'Windy, there's nothing you can announce now that will make any difference.'

But Windy proceeded with the statement he had mentally prepared, 'The young man who calls himself Joey Bud is the son of my son and his name was written in my Bible when he was born, twenty years ago: Joseph Gerard Willoughby, the third.'

Jim Billings commented drily, 'Windy – the dog beat you to it.'

'How could you do such a thing? Deny your own flesh and blood! Your own grandson!' exclaimed Martha.

Windy defended himself, 'No, no, it was not like that. When I denied him I had not recognized him. It was only when he began shouting at me that I recognized Joseph's voice. Then, of course I knew and – came to my senses.'

'But that was two weeks ago!'

'I know I should have returned immediately, but I was frightened. Simply appalled. Can you not understand? My way of life ended. The whole purpose of it

123

stripped from me! Gone forever the life of wandering and searching.'

Martha protested, 'But why be appalled when you have found what you have been searching for? That is surely a cause for rejoicing!'

The Professor tilted his head thoughtfully. 'But which has more power over a man, reality? Or the dream?'

'Reality, of course,' said Martha.

'No, my dear Mrs Heath, not at all, I assure you, for even as this young man was shooting up to six feet in height with the strength to throw a calf over his head with one hand, I was being caught into the dream of imagining that I would find the little lost boy somewhere hereabouts, that I had a right to him, I was his grandfather, and the search for him would give me a goal for the rest of my life.'

'You twist plain facts into lies!' cried Martha. 'Not the faintest regard for the truth!'

'Truth?' But Windy's tone was doubtful and meditative and Martha saw that he was ready with a lecture.

Martha hurried on, 'And what utter selfishness! Real cruelty! No consideration whatever for the suffering you were bringing to those two young people.'

Windy was stung. 'But I have *some* rights! Please remember, I am his grandfather!'

'So you've remembered that at last!' Martha cried. 'After two weeks! It's a wonder you troubled to come back at all. Why did you?'

'It was my conscience,' admitted Windy sadly, 'I couldn't stand it any longer.'

'Again your own selfish feelings! Not a thought for them.'

So many people were listening it was no wonder that Windy became aware of a large audience and in stentorian tones, announced, 'Conscience! As imperative a summons as the alarm clock which wakens a happy dreamer. It would not let me rest. It forced me to return.'

Gilly's audible comment was pure admiration, 'Ain't he nutty!'

'It is a relief,' Windy said, 'a load off my shoulders to know that I have at last done my duty by Joseph's son.'

Martha looked at the old Professor with more gentleness. There was a short silence.

'And now you must get to know each other,' she said kindly.

Jepson said, 'He is a fine fellow. You will be proud of him.'

Windy seemed doubtful. 'Will I? His abuse of the English language – "I ain't never done" – to think that a Willoughby—'

Martha laughed, 'Letty will teach him. And I will help.'

'I trust so,' the Professor said with a sigh. 'Now I think I must be on my way.'

'Why, you can't leave now,' said Martha. 'Of course you will stay for the wedding. Your boy and our girl.'

'You are very kind, Mrs Heath,' said Windy, 'but I think I must go. To tell the truth, I long for the plains. Recent events have been so disturbing—'

'I always told him it would kill him if he ever found that child,' said Jim with a grin.

The moon was no longer sitting on the ground, magnified by the earth's atmosphere into that immense floating ball of gold. It had moved quite a way up the sky.

The band was playing 'When the Merry-go-round Broke Down.'

Letty and Joey were not dancing now.

125

Not holding each other in any way.

They stood side by side but not very close. They were not even looking at each other.

They felt a little shy with each other now that all heaven lay ahead.

Author's Note

Mary O'Hara is a composer by vocation, a writer by avocation. Or perhaps it is the other way around. Her piano studies were the first to achieve publication but her stories, which include *My Friend Flicka,* have gained wider acclaim. At an early age she decided that someday she would combine the two and write a musical. The idea took root. A large box was labelled *For the Musical,* and into it went the music, lyrics, character sketches, story outlines. The actual play could not be written until the locale was chosen, a background out of which the music would naturally flow.

This did not happen until she went to live in Wyoming. There, on the great plains, she found a world different from anything she had ever seen. Vast, silent, empty. A secret and hidden world of incredible beauty. The decision made itself.

She knew it would be a folk tale. Authenticity comes from the earth, the people, and the customs–true Americana. She wrote *The Catch Colt.*

The Catholic University of America, School of Music, produced the musical. The play was then revised and a new orchestration prepared by Hershy Kay.

Dramatists Play Service published the play.

Lastly the author has written the story, extricated from the stage setting.

CHRISTIAN HERALD ASSOCIATION AND ITS MINISTRIES

CHRISTIAN HERALD ASSOCIATION, founded in 1878, publishes The Christian Herald Magazine, one of the leading interdenominational religious monthlies in America. Through its wide circulation, it brings inspiring articles and the latest news of religious developments to many families. From the magazine's pages came the initiative for CHRISTIAN HERALD CHILDREN'S HOME and THE BOWERY MISSION, two individually supported not-for-profit corporations.

CHRISTIAN HERALD CHILDREN'S HOME, established in 1894, is the name for a unique and dynamic ministry to disadvantaged children, offering hope and opportunities which would not otherwise be available for reasons of poverty and neglect. The goal is to develop each child's potential and to demonstrate Christian compassion and understanding to children in need.

Mont Lawn is a permanent camp located in Bushkill, Pennsylvania. It is the focal point of a ministry which provides a healthful "vacation with a purpose" to children who without it would be confined to the streets of the city. Up to 1000 children between the ages of 7 and 11 come to Mont Lawn each year.

Christian Herald Children's Home maintains year-round contact with children by means of an *In-City Youth Ministry*. Central to its philosophy is the belief that only through sustained relationships and demonstrated concern can individual lives be truly enriched. Special emphasis is on individual guidance, spiritual and family counseling and tutoring. This follow-up ministry to inner-city children culminates for many in financial assistance toward higher education and career counseling.

THE BOWERY MISSION, located at 227 Bowery, New York City, has since 1879 been reaching out to the lost men on the Bowery, offering them what could be their last chance to rebuild their lives. Every man is fed, clothed and ministered to. Countless numbers have entered the 90-day residential rehabilitation program at the Bowery Mission. A concentrated ministry of counseling, medical care, nutrition therapy, Bible study and Gospel services awakens a man to spiritual renewal within himself.

These ministries are supported solely by the voluntary contributions of individuals and by legacies and bequests. Contributions are tax deductible. Checks should be made out either to CHRISTIAN HERALD CHILDREN'S HOME or to THE BOWERY MISSION.

Administrative Office: 40 Overlook Drive, Chappaqua, New York 10514
Telephone: (914) 769-9000